FORGET-ME-NOTS

A posy of English memories

FORGET-ME-NOTS
GRAND
A posy of English memories

First published in 1990
by This England Books,
73 Rodney Road, Cheltenham, Gloucestershire

Printed in Great Britain by
BPCC Wheatons Ltd, Exeter

ISBN 0 906324 15 7

Contents

Foreword	*Roy Faiers*	8
On the Road with Donkey Jack	*Olive Willis*	11
The Saturday Penny	*Enid Dunlop*	15
English Heaven	*Mary Waters*	17
All the Fun of the Fair	*Doreen Barfield*	20
Bliss	*L. Darley Forward*	25
Pimlico Market	*Gilbert H. Fabes*	26
Trees for my Grandchildren	*Rosemary Jenkins*	30
Together	*Veronica Medd*	33
The Corner Sweetshop	*Eric R. Joy*	34
The Button Box	*F.A. Joyce*	39
The Old Mill	*John Harris*	40
Bathing at Bude	*Claire McLachlan*	41
September is a Gypsy	*Margaret Greenhalgh*	43
For What We Are About to Receive	*Doreen Barfield*	44
The Empty Pocket	*Joan Primrose Wells*	49
Our Medicine Cupboard	*Hazel Cottam*	50
Gold and Silver Memories	*Cicely Smith*	53
The Store Cupboard	*Peggy Winckworth*	54
Our Diamond Day	*George Pearson*	57
Our Village Flower Show	*John Dunford*	58
Railway Children	*Anne Marie Edwards*	62
Our English Isle	*Esme Vernon*	66
Hallelujah and Salmon Sandwiches	*W.M. Hopewell*	68
The Sampler	*Doris Seys Price*	76
Hidden Treasures	*Cicely Smith*	79
Mushroom Magic	*Gee Tennent*	80
Michaelmas Daisies	*Salter Fox*	83
Do You Remember 1926?	*Elsie Gadsby*	84
Country Blood	*J. Sturgess*	86
Washday in the 1920s	*Hazel Cottam*	88
Country Fashion	*Dorothy Mary Wade*	93
Going Shopping	*Frank Railton*	94
The Old Apple Room	*Elizabeth Royston*	98
Cycling to Court	*T.J. Aspley*	102
Team Work	*Cynthia Haefli-Wells*	106
A Treasury	*Muriel Hilton*	107
A Village Christmas	*Pauline Grain*	108
Song of the Donkey	*Harry Broughton*	113
Easter Memories	*Doreen Barfield*	114
Nowadays	*C. Holmes*	117
Harvest Holiday	*Betty Morris*	118
Progress?	*Hilda Gee*	121
The Sunday Outing	*Ron Collier*	122

Foreword

by Roy Faiers, Editor of "This England"

The wind was a torrent of darkness amid the gusty trees,
The moon was a ghostly galleon tossed upon cloudy seas,
The road was a ribbon of moonlight over the purple moor,
And the highwayman came riding—riding—riding
The highwayman came riding, up to the old inn-door.

In the Thirties, as a knobbly-kneed little lad bedecked in school cap, blazer and tie, I mounted the stage in a village concert to deliver a recitation of this adventure-packed poem by Alfred Noyes which I had been committing to parrot memory for the previous month or so. I can hardly think now that my piping voice truly conveyed the increasing level of excitement as the daring brigand came riding, riding, riding to meet Bess, the landlord's black-eyed daughter, but the rustic audience of parents and offspring, relatives and friends, were sufficiently interested in the rhyming tale to stop fidgeting long enough in the stifling heat of the parish hall to listen and later to reward my bumbling performance with a ripple of applause. From that day on, I not only warmed towards poetry in general but also to Alfred Noyes in particular, who has ever remained at the top of my long list of favourites.

Many years later I had the good fortune to visit the poet's home on the Isle of Wight, where he died in 1958, and I discovered how deeply he respected the blessing of memory in his life. On one occasion in May 1937, Alfred Noyes was asked to speak to an audience of 8,000 young people from all parts of what we then called the Empire, in the Albert Hall, London, and he told them of the great part that remembrance would one day play in their lives. Though spoken more than half a century ago, his words seem uncannily apt for the youth of today. This is part of what he said:

"You are confronted today by a world that has lost something; a world that in the rush and roar of its daily life has no time for recollection; and has almost ceased to believe in real values, or is engaged in falsifying them and confusing the lines of right and wrong.

"Youth is enviable, not because it sees further than its elders, but because it has time to learn from the past, and even from the mistakes of the past. Mankind is in desperate need of that vital knowledge, the knowledge of the things that belong to its real peace. These things are clearly written in every

unspoiled memory. Follow them in simple truth; trust to the hand that wrote them there, and it may be that yours will be the generation chosen to redeem a war-shattered world."

I would love to have been one of those youngsters in the Albert Hall that day, though I fear that much of what the great poet had to say would have been quickly lost as more exciting thoughts crowded into my young mind. But now, oh yes, now I would listen and devour every word he said. For now I can corroborate his view that as the years roll by we learn so much from recalling our past experiences — not just the great, momentous happenings but also those little everyday occurrences that burrow deep into our memories . . . the kindly action of a stranger, the biting word of a friend; the toys we played with; the homes we lived in; the corner shop; the sweets we bought; the postman, policeman, doctor and vicar. The list is endless, for the tapestry of life is made up of so many varied threads.

Since memory is such a great entertainer, there is a bonus waiting for all of us as we grow older. Because in addition to our own memories, there is enjoyment to be had in reading about the minor experiences of others, many of which find an echo in our own lives and set off a trigger of personal reminiscences that, until then, we had thought lost forever. It was with this in mind that, when we began publishing *This England* more than 22 years ago, a section of the magazine was devoted to readers recounting their recollections from the England of yesteryear. We called the feature "Forget-Me-Nots" and it is from the many accounts we have received and published over the years that the 40 or so essays and poems in this book are drawn. You will be able to trot down the road with "Donkey Jack", pop in for a dip while "Bathing at Bude", re-live the delights of browsing at "Pimlico Market", and join the chapel outing in "Hallelujah and Salmon Sandwiches".

To those who may doubt the value of recalling memories from childhood, perhaps believing that we should turn our back on the past and look only to the future, let me quote again from the words of Alfred Noyes on that day in 1937 when speaking to the youth of Britain:

"Remembrance is as vital to nations as to men. It not only prevents us from losing the real values of the past, but it infinitely increases the worth of our own lives here and now."

So, if you're quite ready, I invite you to sit back, relax, and turn the pages of this little book as you take a trip with me down that leafy avenue called "Forget-Me-Not Lane" . . .

On the road with 'DONKEY JACK'

We were proud of our "Donkey Jack", for besides being the pet of the family he was our usual mode of transport. In the shafts of his high-wheeled-donkey cart, with his polished leather harness and bright brasses, he provided us with stately transport indeed, and with large gig umbrella, silver-topped whip handle, and warm-lined leather cart rug, we were prepared for anything. We needed to be, for many a sharp thunderstorm caught us during our travels and as Donkey Jack made very slow progress in a thunderstorm these useful articles were a real necessity.

Usually he was very good and took us to market or visiting distant friends on neighbouring farms. He took us for "nutting" in Honey Pot Wood; he took us to country lanes where blackberries grew in abundance, but best of all he took us all the way to visit Granny — the great distance of eight miles.

A winter ride to Granny's we well remember. All in our Sunday-best warm winter coats, high lace-up boots and long black woollen stockings, furry hats, gloves, and

muffs for our hands, and huge thick scarves almost as large as blankets wrapped and pinned around each one of us — we were well prepared for our journey.

For family outings, an extra seat was fixed in the rear of the cart, so we travelled back-to-back, parents in front and children behind. We started off in high spirits, but because it was a frosty morning and the roads were treacherous, Donkey Jack made slow progress. In spite of Dad's skilled guidance with the reins and Donkey Jack's keen road sense in avoiding the slippery patches, we could only make walking pace, for it was too dangerous to trot. Many ponies suffered broken knees in this kind of weather, but Dad was too careful and patient to risk a fallen horse or donkey. He preferred them to go at their own safe pace rather than urge them on into accidents. However, our progress was so slow that we older children preferred to get out and walk while Dad led Donkey Jack until we came to the village blacksmith's, only open on a Sunday for real emergencies.

The blacksmith's always held great interest for us. The strong swarthy men who wielded the hammers were bronzed and glazed with sweat as they hammered the red-hot iron into shape. It was always a hive of industry; ploughshares to sharpen and repair, iron hoops for waggon wheels to be welded, broken axles for repair, link chains to be mended, and a constant stream of horses being led to the blacksmith's for a renewal of their iron shoes. Row upon row of iron shoes hung up in the blacksmith's shop, but every horse and every foot had to be carefully fitted. So the smithy's furnace was always kept red-hot with specially hard steam coal, and a hand on the pumping bellows would bring it up to a yet more glowing heat. The shoe was held carefully between long-handled tongs in the searing heat until it became red-hot and pliable. Then it was put to the anvil and beaten hard into shape, plunged into cooling water and fitted to the waiting horse's hoof. Did it fit, was it exactly right for this horse? If not, the whole procedure of heating and hammering and shaping would be repeated, again and again if necessary, for the blacksmith was a craftsman and proud of his skill.

But Donkey Jack did not need new shoes this time, he only needed "roughing" and this was done by the blacksmith simply screwing into his iron shoes some spiked nails, thereby enabling him to trot on the slippery roads without slipping and falling. The job done, we loaded up and proceeded on our way.

The church bells pealed out and seemed to welcome us on our way. We were always happy to hear those bells for then we knew we were halfway there, halfway to Granny's. Passing through an expanse of common land, where Donkey Jack would want to stop and make acquaintance with another friendly donkey, we knew that at last our journey was coming to an end. We could smell the newly-baked bread from the baker's shop and our hearts missed a beat, for this was another sign that we

were almost there. Not that the baker baked on Sundays, but for six days a week he did and that delicious aroma of home-baked bread always pervaded the place.

Nearing the village pond we were welcomed, startled and frightened all in one, by the villagers' huge flock of geese that always stood sentinel as if guarding their village from strangers. How they hissed and cackled and breathed out threats and warnings. But we overcame our fears because just behind this pond lived Granny. We really had arrived. As we opened the door, there she sat as usual in her little corner seat, almost doubled up with arthritis but always busy with her hands. In summer it would be shelling peas or slicing beans; in winter an everlasting pile of socks and stockings was before her to darn, for she lived with her farmer son and daughter and a host of grandchildren who always needed their woollen stockings darned.

Wearing a shawl about her shoulders, with a little lace and purple velvet cap perched jauntily upon her head above her thin wispy hair, she wrinkled her apple-pink face into a cheerful smile as we all trooped in.

"Well my old sugars, come to see Granny?"

"Yes" we all answered. "Donkey Jack brought us."

OLIVE WILLIS

The Saturday Penny

In these days when the lowest sum to offer a child as pocket money appears to be 25 or even 50 new pence it seems almost fantastic to recall the old "penny a week" allowance of pre-1914 days! Yet there was nothing poverty-stricken or niggardly about that modest copper — its spending power was quite high — and it was considered ample revenue for a small girl of six or seven — as I was then.

I had a little friend who received the same amount from her father — the manager of a bank in the small country town in which we both lived — and as we usually played together on Saturday mornings it became the welcome custom that each father should produce a penny for the other child as well as his own. This, we felt, was affluence indeed — and Saturday became a red-letter day, with a wonderful routine which seldom varied. We would hang about in full view of my father until he emerged sufficiently from the paper to realise the day of the week, and the necessity of searching his pockets for a couple of pennies. And I may say that four halfpennies were never quite the same thing. Having thanked him politely — and we had to be careful about this — we hurried up the street to the bank to draw the second half of our dividend.

With our small noses just reaching the top of the polished counter we watched, fascinated, while the cashiers scooped up piles of glittering sovereigns into copper shovels and casually tipped them into drawers, and used beautiful glass weights to balance the chinking bags of silver on the scales. Then the Manager would spot us from his inner sanctum and issue majestically forth to roll two bright new pennies into our expectant hands.

A few pleasantries were exchanged and we backed our way out of the swing doors to run helter-skelter for that Mecca of all Meccas, the toy shop.

Sixty years ago there was hardly any traffic in a small country town — and no crowds, no hurry or bustle, in the shops. Children could take all the morning, if they wished, to choose a penny toy — and there were shelves of them on which to feast the eyes.

What bliss it was! Should one buy the mechanical clown who turned somersaults? . . . or some coloured beads — there was a large box for a penny? Perhaps a really beautifully-made piece of furniture for the doll's house . . . or what about that green tin frog — with yards of thread attached by an elastic band to its underneath so that it progressed along the ground in lively fashion as one pulled or slackened the string . . . how difficult it was to decide!

We were always allowed to wind up everything mechanical, play everything musical, and generally test each article thoroughly to help us make up our minds — which, looking back, seems extraordinarily kind when

English Heaven

Our land has scenes serene
Lush beauty fresh and green
Which peace and health impart
Here in my English heart.

Here we can take our place
In history's onward race
Wherever else we roam
Here in my English home.

Each season's beauty glows
And summer's glory shows
All that our land has given
Here in my English heaven.

MARY WATERS

only a penny purchase from each of us was to be the business transacted! But that was the way of things when shops were private concerns and when those in charge knew all their regular customers — even down to their children — and there was plenty of time for everyone.

Each clutching his choice of the week, and each with half his income gone, we hurried to our last port of call — the sweet shop kept by three ladies of three different generations. Would our luck be in and the oldest of the three be on duty at the counter? Grannie Walton's eyes were dim and the scales had to tip very decidedly before she observed them do so. As a result one often secured

two or three extra sweets — over and above the four ounces a penny which was already the good value of the times.

What lovely colours Cupid's Whispers were! — and the endearing messages they bore always had an astonishing effect when handed round the kitchen, producing screams and giggles and violent nudgings! How delectable, too, the bootlaces of liquorice — which could be torn off in strips — the pink and white sugar mice — and chocolate drops covered with hundreds and thousands, many of which would drop off in the bag and be tipped into the mouth as a final bonne-bouche.

Then there was sherbet — taken dry, to fizz delightfully in the mouth — coconut chips, pink and white, of great chewing quality — round glycerine lozenges which

— when sucked — had the added attraction of adhering firmly to both persons and things and could be used on seats with fascinating results.

Honeysuckle Twist — a revolting brown, glutinous coil — never appealed to us at all, though no doubt it had its buyers, neither did brandy balls nor anything flavoured with aniseed. Highly-coloured red and yellow pear-drops left our tongues such startling shades as to horrify my mother, but sugar candy — with its bit of string through the middle (be sure you don't swallow it, dear!) — and satin cushions — now known by the grander name of pralines — were considered very proper sweets to buy.

When, in years to come, my pocket money soared to the staggering height of sixpence a week my earning powers likewise increased. I could weed the drive at sixpence an hour, said my father . . . go round the shops and pay the weekly books for tuppence, suggested my mother — and this last usually had further inducements, in the shape of an orange from the grocer and a "farthing change" reel of cotton or packet of pins from the draper.

Perhaps my most lucrative "job" was to work the hand-blower in a neighbouring village church while the youngest of my three big brothers practised the organ for a solid hour. This brought a reward as much as fourpence — of which I usually mortgaged half for the purpose of supplying myself with sweets to help while away the tedium of 60 long minutes pumping up and down.

Christmas and birthdays were of course highlights in our financial year. From the golden half-sovereign of our extreme youth we were raised to a whole golden pound, which my father would place under a plate or saucer at breakfast as a time-honoured joke — and be rewarded by our delighted discovery. I doubt if any modern child gets quite the same thrill as we did from our humble penny, which was worth all its four precious farthings.

ENID DUNLOP

All the Fun of the Fair

When I was a teenager a highlight of my school holidays was a visit to Barnet Horse Fair, granted by a Royal Charter dating back over seven hundred years, and held for three consecutive September days in two fields beside the Great North Road, close to the London North Eastern Railway line. The last time I went there was in 1929 when my mother and I walked over from Totteridge. The sounds from the Fun Fair became louder as we made our way along the almost-country road, and our pace quickened as our excitement grew. Soon shouts from the horse field could be distinguished from the blaring music of the steam calliopes. From the sloping fields rose a cloud of dust, stirred up by the horses and milling crowds,

The Horse Fair was our first love. The scents of warm horseflesh, old leather, ammonia and baled straw evoked country days worlds away from London, its skyline a shimmering blur to the south. Droves of New Forest ponies, fresh from their wild woodland, were herded by colourful characters wearing bright neckerchiefs. As we watched a horse being put through its paces, shown off to a prospective buyer by being led at a gallop up and down the field, accompanied by much screaming and shouting as it plunged and bucked, the same thing was happening behind our backs so we were in danger of being trampled on, which added to the thrill.

Elderly men, wearing stocks with loud pins, and green-mouldy bowlers, clasped hands to confirm a sale, forever binding. In the centre of the field all was noise, flying hooves and dust, while round the sides nosebags were tossed, straw-sucking grooms lazed beside their charges in the shade, and the cheapjacks, each with his little knot of spectators, kept up their lines of patter or barked their wares.

These gentlemen always fascinated me. There was a glass-cutter who demonstrated his emery cutting-wheel, slicing strips off a piece of glass like a hot knife going through butter. Alas, having purchased one, it seemed very blunt when used at home, but perhaps I did not have the knack. The ventriloquist with his wooden dummy sitting on his knee entertained a few onlookers, but when it was time to pass his cap around, the audience faded away.

Donald the Scot, defying strangulation, distended his neck muscles like knotted rope while strong volunteers played tug-of-war with his head in a noose between them. His partner went round shaking a hat amongst us while Donald, in singlet and kilt, staggered about, scarlet of face, looking ready to collapse. I considered his efforts worth a threepenny bit, and when the last ha'penny had been dunned from the watching crowd he went into some further contortions, then the act was over and Donald staggered to the running-board of his dilapidated car, where he sat swigging beer.

On one memorable occasion we saw two detectives pounce on a "Find the Lady" exponent and march him off the field. Then there was the man who sold rolled gold watches with a pound note thrown in for the lucky buyer, or was it a confederate? We passed on to the seller of corn cure and hair-restorer, whose missing front teeth made his sibilant patter worthy of mimicry when we were home.

Often we were the only females in the horse field, a

man's world, fast dying as spreading London made it more difficult each year to bring through the herds of wild ponies on the hoof, and the demand for draught horses grew less. But year by year the Fun Fair grew noisier and brighter as electric lights blazed, outlining the booths, while the music blared. As everything became more mechanical, so the individuality of the rides was lost; even the flashy young men, surefooted as they made their way between the gaily-coloured horses on the roundabouts collecting fares, seemed all alike with oiled quiffs and drooping cigarettes.

Only around the edges of the field lingered individuals not yet driven away by the mechanical age. My mother was a great consulter of palmists and crystal-ball gazers; she was ready to chat to them and sample them all. Once we were invited into the caravan home of a gypsy woman, one of the Lee tribe, whose members attended fairs all over the country. I hung back; I was more at home with rough horse-copers than these persistent ladies who wanted their palms crossed with silver, called us "ducks" or "dearie", and talked a lot of nonsense to the gullible. I need not have worried. The caravan was spotless, and Gypsy Lee a pleasant woman who let me look at her collection of Toby jugs which covered two shelves along the side of the caravan, one of the old-fashioned horse-drawn kind, brightly painted with garlands.

We did the round of side-shows, watching a troupe of cowboys doing rope-spinning and knife-throwing tricks; the Indian Fakir, obviously a negro under his turban; and for threepence one could gaze at the Fat Lady, a girl of nineteen with a pretty face lost in rolls of fat, a wreath of tired artificial roses on her soft, fair hair. There were only three of us in the tent to listen to her manager who gave her dimensions and waved a huge pair of her bloomers at us. The boxing booths had their challengers to all-comers, skipping and shadow-boxing on a platform outside, ready to toss a pair of gloves to any stalwart who fancied his prowess.

We wandered past the shooting-galleries and coconut-shies, sampled hot pies, ginger snaps, and sucked the translucent coating from toffee-apples which were always too green and bitter to eat. We listened to a barker extolling the beauties of his collection of "living statuary" inside the tent, and watched a contortionist going through her act. Then there was the Mysterious Mummy; the showman, dressed in sola topi and shorts, stood beside a coffin which held a dusty, desiccated body supposed to be hundreds of years old. The men in the audience were asked to remove their hats in the presence of the dead, while a negro played muffled drum-rolls and another prayed, making obeisance at the foot of the coffin.

Our last call was always at the stall where, amid flashing lights, model aircraft flew round above the players'

heads. When sufficient tickets had been sold each holder was allotted a plane, which travelled over a numbered chart below. As the planes were in flight each player pulled a lever that released a spiked "bomb" which dropped onto the chart. The object was to score the highest number which was at the end of the chart farthest from the start of the flight. Everyone pulled their levers as soon as the aircraft were in motion, but as an old habitué of fairgrounds I had learnt that if I "held my fire" while I counted up to three I would most probably win. The prize was always the same, a flat tin of indifferent toffees, a half-layer padded out with paper shavings, yet another useful container for my cigarette card collection.

As the afternoon wore on activity in the horse field ceased, while at sunset the Fun Fair came into its own as crowds flocked to its bright lights and hypnotic sounds. It was time for us to walk home; the sky glowed brightly above the fairground, while its mixture of rumbustious tunes, made enchanting by distance, followed us along the road. Like so many before us down the ages, we had spent a happy day at Barnet Fair.

DOREEN BARFIELD

Bliss . . .

Summer: and dreams of holiday delights.
To fly? To cruise? To swim in tropic sea?
No; none of these sing siren songs for me,
Nor crowded foreign tours "to see the sights".
My course is set. Old clothes, a light rucksack,
Leisure and peace to wander where I will,
Through wood and meadow, over breezy hill,
To follow hidden path or moorland track.

The bracing whip of steely-shafted rain,
Life-giving touch of sunshine's glowing hand,
Tall, wind-beruffled trees, wide pastureland,
The crisping plume of richly swollen grain,
Quiet friendliness of rivers' laggard flow —
These are my joys; with lark-song overhead
Leading me like a falling silver thread
To hoist my pack and gaily onward go.

L. DARLEY FORWARD

Pimlico Market

I recall the pictures of a bygone age in the Warwick Street Market, Pimlico, at the turn of the century, with its stalls and itinerant vendors.

Father had his pitch with an electric machine mounted on a box, covered with green baize and containing wet batteries, upon three old perambulator wheels. The machine had two polished brass pillars supporting a dial, to register the strength of the current, which was transmitted into four brass handles. These were held in pairs by the customers, and men would vie with others to get the indicating needle to the highest point. A party of three or more could be accommodated by those outside holding a handle each and connecting up hand to hand with one or more in between them, the current in circuit through all. If a party consisted of two or more young girls the resulting screams and laughter attracted a crowd of interested onlookers.

Wet Saturday nights cut Father's takings from an average of five shillings (a lot in those days), to the detriment of the household income. On bank holidays he took the machine to Battersea Park or Clapham Common and good takings on these days were reflected on the following Sunday, if he took us on a steamer trip from Westminster to Greenwich in the afternoon. A certain public house in Greenwich was allowed to stay open to supply refreshment to "bonafide" travellers only. Each customer was asked two questions: "Where've you come from?" and "Did you sleep there last night?" The regulations having been adhered to, the load from the paddle steamer gave many non-voyagers the opportunity to join the queue for the sweetest of all beverages, a pint out of hours.

Bank holidays gave me my first incentive for commercialism, when I was old enough to relieve Father temporarily, to work his machine and take money from customers. Schoolboys at a halfpenny a go seemed to be attracted by my managerial capacity on those occasions, and I was very proud if, on Father's return, the takings were worthy of his trust.

There are many memories of the Warwick Street Market in those days and I particularly remember the two ice-cream "Jacks": Antonio Garcia and Marcia Mareno.

Antonio's pitch was across the street to Father's. He was the cheap "Jack" who sold flavoured water ices, from a farthing to a penny, standing on an upturned box, always puffing an old clay pipe. When the weather was hot and business was good, he beamed with pleasure. His friendly smile and typical Italian fondness of children made him popular with his poor young customers. A request of "Give us a taster, Jack", was seldom refused, and a morsel of ice on a large wooden spoon gave satisfaction to a ragged recipient. On the side of his dowdy barrow was a scrawled notice painted in red and blue which read:

I, Antonio Garcia, vendor of ice-cream, 9, Little Collidge Street,
will give £2 to anyone who Proves my Vendings unpure.

Marcia Mareno's pitch, higher up the street, indicated

his superiority with a brightly-painted green and gold notice:

Guarantee of Purity.
I, Marcia Moreno of 6, Little College Court, will give a reward of £10, to anyone who can prove my ice-cream impure.

His stall had four highly-polished brass slender pillars and he wore a clean white apron, but his prices were too high for the poor children, being from twopence to sixpence for "Real Cream Ices".

Marcia's manners were impeccable, and his servility to his better class customers was typical of his race. His very movements had an artistry worthy of portrayal by any master painter of the Italian school, but a request of "Give us a taster" was met by a haughty look of disdain.

The Salvation Army Band was always a Saturday night attraction to the street kids. Their curiosity was aroused when the drum was placed in the centre of the circle, and coins were thrown, in case a badly-aimed penny came rolling through the darkness to be picked up "for keeps".

Another possible source of income to a street kid was the black man with gleaming white teeth, who gave a halfpenny to the boy who submitted to having his teeth cleaned to prove the marvellous powers of the tooth powder. The young assistant's head was held back while the man using his forefinger cleaned the boy's teeth. A remarkable transformation was at once evident. The teeth became gleaming white, a non-permanent "whitening" having been applied surreptitiously!

The lavender-sellers drifted through "our street" with their melodious song:

Come and buy, my sweet blooming lavender
There are sixteen blue branches a penny.
You'll buy them once, you'll buy them twice:
They make your clothes smell very nice.

The coalmen shouted loudly, "Co-a-ll!" (at £1 a ton) with one hand placed at the side of the face, covering an ear, as if it hurt.

The muffin man's bell was a merry sound on a Sunday afternoon with his goods on a large wooden tray, covered with a clean white cloth and green baize, on his head. He was neatly dressed and wore a white or green baize apron to match the tray of muffins and crumpets, wholesome, delectable and fresh, at five for twopence.

The knife-grinder with his "spark-machine" was a great attraction to the kids. He seemed oblivious to danger as sparks from the grinding stone flew around his hands, and magically disappeared while he treadled the mechanism of his cumbersome contraption, supported by a large wheel and two legs.

My own experiences of London street life, if repeated in detail, would cover many more pages, but the particular environment of my own street and neighbourhood is the canvas upon which my picture is painted.

GILBERT H. FABES

Trees for my grandchildren

At a garden centre I overheard a charming feminine voice saying, "I'm planting trees for my grandchildren — fruit trees, mainly, because the blossom is so lovely."

My thoughts chased back over the years to the carefree days of my childhood, for my grandfather planted an orchard as well as landscaping a delightful garden. And it was the orchard — not the mature walled garden — that his grandchildren and great-grandchildren enjoyed so much, although we each inherited his green fingers and put them to good use.

In the spring we dashed out to pick the snowdrops, primroses and violets which abounded in the hedgerow forming part of the boundary of the orchard and there were masses of daffodils under the fruit trees — "King Alfred" predominating amongst "Emperor" and "Empress". Later, bluebells mingled with the hedge's fresh green beech leaves and the pear and apple blossom was superb against blue and white skies — drifts of pink and white petals turning the orchard into fairyland.

Around Easter there were fluffy yellow chicks under the apple trees. One particular hen, known affectionately as Alice, because she came to the kitchen door, could always find a way through some gap in the hedge from the field where she could roam freely but she much preferred to take her brood on a voyage of discovery down the orchard paths.

During the summer holidays a swing was attached to the lowest branch of the tallest pear tree and what fun we had swinging higher and higher. My adventurous cousins climbed all the trees, starting on the nursery slopes of the Bramley Seedlings and finishing at the summit of the pear tree. I was the only grand-daughter, the book-worm who invariably sat reading happily on a branch of a very small apple tree on sunny afternoons.

Towards the end of the holidays we helped to pick the pear crop and the small sweet yellow eating apples with rosy cheeks, whose name I cannot now recall, only the delicious flavour. And current catalogues do not bring the name to mind. We gathered bright red Siberian crab apples and helped to strain the liquid after they were boiled through a jelly bag. We printed labels painstakingly and finally stored the richly-coloured jelly in the spacious pantry. Bramley Seedlings weighing between eight and twelve ounces made mouth-watering apple pies. We plucked luscious blackberries from the orchard's hedges for bramble jelly. After a September gale we competed to see who could collect the most windfalls and my mother made jelly from the assortment of fruit using late raspberries or blackberries for flavouring. In October the last of the apples were ripe — the crisp eating apples that had excellent keeping qualities and these we laid carefully, so that none touched, on the shelves in the cool cellar whose stone-flagged floor was already covered with newspapers upon which lay pound after pound of large green cooking apples.

The plum trees bore fruit most erratically. In 1939, however, they obligingly gave a bumper crop. We picked them during the fateful September weekend when the Second World War began and we made a useful quantity of jam before rationing started. Why so much jam? In those days my mother made delicious crusty bread and home-made preserves helped the meagre butter ration to go further.

Sadly, the plum picking was the last occasion on which all the grandchildren were to be together. My adventurous cousins joined the Royal Air Force and I picked the remainder of the fruit with the help of a boy from the village who simply revelled in climbing trees.

Throughout the Second World War the great-grandchildren played contentedly in the orchard — soon they will be driving their sporty cars along the fast lane of the Motorway that has long been scheduled to overwhelm the orchard, across the very spot where the pear tree's lowest branch carried my swing. Nevertheless, I enjoy recollecting that for more than half a century the orchard rang with children's voices and generations of kittens frisked and gambolled in the grass, and I am thankful that the grandfather I never knew gave me such joy throughout my childhood. Recently, when visiting the eldest great-grandchild, I found him planting fruit trees around his new house with his sturdy four-year-old son trying very hard to help him. Tradition lives on and drifts of blossom make an English spring unforgettably beautiful.

ROSEMARY JENKINS

Together

Today the young men's visions
Are not the old men's dreams.
The young now want no part or lot
Within their parents' schemes.

Perhaps because some dreams came true,
And turned so soon to dust,
There seems so little need to strive
For what is right or just.

Their expectations have been raised;
No need to slave or save:
The Welfare State will care for all
From cradle to the grave.

Yet young men need their visions still,
For dreams the old men long;
Together striving for the weak,
Together they are strong.

VERONICA MEDD

The Corner Sweetshop

One day I am determined to go back and measure myself against the red brick wall that flanked the pavement and encircled the garden at the rear of Ellis's corner sweetshop, which in my younger days seemed to tower above me like some impregnable fortress. As a schoolboy, choked with a celluloid collar, and complete with dickey bow, short trousers, dirty knees and the inevitable down-wrinkling socks, I would play marbles in front of it, bounce an old tennis ball for hours on its surface, decorate it in white chalk with intertwined hearts and arrows proclaiming the latest street romance, or just lean idly against it with my companions exchanging cigarette cards or planning our next orchard-robbing expedition.

It was over this wall that we lost many of the youthful accessories which represented to us the joys of living. Schoolboys cling tenaciously to their wordly possessions and if we had the misfortune to lose, over the wall, any of our kites, balls or wire-tipped arrows, we would set a scheme into operation rivalling in tactics the best laid schemes of any field marshal of the day.

Two boys, like Trojans of old, would crouch side by side with backs bent beneath the wall, making a platform upon which I as one of the lightest would be hoisted. With a hobnailed boot boring into each unflinching back and with hot, sticky fingers pressed against the brickwork I would slowly extend my body until my eyes were looking over the top layer of brickwork to ascertain if Mr. Ellis, seizing a moment from his shopkeeping duties, was there bending and grunting between the rows of his sad-looking cabbages or the serried ranks of his wilting carrots.

Past experience had taught us at this stage of the operation to be extremely cautious. It had not been unknown for over-zealous scouts to receive well-directed clods of earth full in the face from the irate Mr. Ellis who always somehow seemed to guess our intentions each time we appeared dramatically above the top level of his wall.

We had learnt, too, that if he did see us he would comb the garden for our treasures and from that point in time we would never see them again. If on the other hand he was engaged in the shop making the paper cups that would later hold our purchases of sherbet, bull's eyes or toffee, mental note would be made of the location of each article for an after-dark sortie amongst his vegetables. Later that evening several modest and unsung heroes, seizing the moment when passing clouds veiled the drifting moon, would scale the heights, drop to the soil beneath and in a twinkling would be back with balls, arrows, kites or windmills, leaving the fuming shopkeeper pondering the next morning over the unexplained but definite footmarks between the drooping vegetation.

No one in his right senses would have ever dreamed of befronting him in his corner empire of sherbet suckers and periodicals to ask openly for the return of our treasures. It would have been courting immediate disaster if not sudden death.

Faced with a question of this nature by some unsuspecting newcomer to the district, the huge grey-flannelled, spectacled figure would erupt suddenly into volcanic action. Snatching at the nearest *John Bull* or *London Illustrated* with a speed rivalling the poisoned darts of the

pygmies, he would belabour the astonished victim about head and shoulders until, like Napoleon, he would beat a hasty and strategic retreat out into the street.

Even if engaged in the legitimate business of spending our Saturday penny, we approached the battle area with extreme alertness. A clanging bell over the inside of the door announced our arrival in a manner similar to that of a boxer entering a ring. Stepping inside we would stand quietly, surrounded by glass jars containing Sherbert Fountains, Gob Stoppers, Liquorice Braid, Jelly Babies and Dolly Mixtures before a counter laden with current copies of *Tiger Tim's Weekly, Lot-o-fun, Rainbows, Titbits,* and a few forlorn copies of the unsold morning papers.

Suddenly, heralded by the shaking of the entire premises, we knew he was coming. As we nervously watched, his great hulk, his balding head, his eternally dripping nose adorned with gold-framed spectacles would emerge through the shaking strings of a beaded curtain that separated shop from living quarters. His huge frame, supported in down-at-heel carpet slippers, would shuffle along between an avenue of dusty glass showcases and a wall festooned with cards displaying pencils, pens, split rings, babies' dummies, tooth-brushes and small bottles of olive oil, until at last he would arrive, gasping but in full command, behind the counter.

This was the moment for which we had rehearsed ourselves before daring to venture inside. Having pressed our little noses for an immeasurable time against his window to ascertain and memorise the four farthings' worth of the sweets we required, we knew we would be courting disaster and a scene, if we dared forget. We would have been repeating it like a litany to ourselves even up to the time of his arrival behind the magazines.

Mr. Ellis hated dithering. It was only by reason of the fact that our hot little fingers were clutching a coin of the realm which he wished transferred to his till, that our presence was even tolerated.

The transaction must now be made at all speed.

In no time, providing your memory was working at full blast, you would be outside again on the pavement clutching four paper bags of screwed up sweetmeats.

There were rare occasions when it was my unhappy duty to present myself to Mr. Ellis for the purchase of a twopenny cane. It was the type of cane sometimes seen and very often felt in many a home in the first quarter of the century. My father, a kindly man but nevertheless a strict parent, always kept one hanging on the picture behind his seat at table and it was amazing how rapidly family squabbles would dissolve during meal times by the mere laying of this cane beside his plate.

The folly of childhood is such that occasionally if both

parents were absent we would have the mad idea of bringing all punishment to an end by the annexation and destruction of the weapon of punishment.

God and my father were not mocked! Nothing was said until the next family outbreak. Without remarking on the missing cane, he would send the troublemaker along to Mr. Ellis's with tuppence for the purpose of a replacement. Mr. Ellis, apart from being a child monster, was I am sure quite psychic for he would instantly add further humiliation to the scene by saying, as he passed the cane over, "So! You've been a bad lad again, have you?"

Worse was yet to come! You must now hastily stuff the cane down your trousers and button your jacket over for fear that the lads of the street should see the instrument of torture and accompany you to your very doorstep with unkind boyish jests about your forthcoming chastisement.

Times have certainly changed! Today, I find myself inspecting one of the comparatively new twopenny pieces thinking that there was once a time when its face value would have taken me eight times into Mr. Ellis's shop to come away each time with a paper coneful of sweets, the like of which, I am sure, we shall never see again!

ERIC R. JOY

The Button Box

We didn't have a button box,
So Mother found a tin
That once contained a pound of tea
To keep the buttons in.

Buttons by the score she had,
Of every size and shape.
Amongst the souvenirs I see
Some beads from Grandma's cape.

Pearl buttons from our baby clothes,
Round buttons from our boots,
Linen ones from Father's shirts,
Brace buttons from his suits.

With the buttons red and blue
I see a shining ring,
A broken brooch, a tiny key,
What memories they bring.

F.A. JOYCE

THE OLD MILL

I know a place
Beside a stream,
A peaceful place,
With silver gleam.

And quiet sounds,
And gentle flow —
And to this place
I often go.

The beauty there
Beside the mill
With healing peace
The heart can fill.
And always, when
I come from there,
The world is bright
With vanished care.

JOHN HARRIS

BATHING at BUDE

Bude was our Mecca for summer holidays, not least because we shared a house with cousins at West Cliff while more cousins had a house nearby. All three families met on the shore for the morning bathe when the tide was low and left behind deep pools which made for safe bathing. These were surrounded by tall rocks that gave seclusion for the older children to don bathing costumes out of sight of prying eyes; the smaller ones were undressed, eventually towelled dry and re-dressed, for all the world to see. Of course, we were clad in warm, one-piece costumes, arms covered to the elbows, legs to the knees, red and white or navy and white striped, boys and girls alike; the girls wore mackintosh mob caps to keep their long hair dry.

Bathing in those days was a ceremony superintended by parents and governess or nurse, and carefully timed. There was no question of putting on our bathing outfits before going to the shore, or spending the morning in and out of the water according to inclination, while sunbathing itself was unheard of. After our bathe we had to run up and down the sands to get warm and were given a currant bun to eat. Then with skirts tucked into our knickers we built a castle to defend against the incoming tide — with all the children and probably a grown-up or two co-opted, it was some castle! Or it might be a fortress inside which we climbed and feverishly patched its walls as the sea broke them down.

It was often a wild sea at Bude with strong currents, and at times bathing in the sea proper was forbidden. Stalwart local women patrolled the shore line barefooted, dressed in long black skirts turned up in front and pinned together at their backs, ready to go to the help of too daring adults. I don't think any of us children could swim except with one foot on the sand, yelling "Look! I can swim". I certainly only learnt to swim years later when I was at Cheltenham Ladies' College, whither we all in turn gravitated.

After lunch the littlest ones had to rest for an hour but a cousin and I were allowed onto the sands alone, no doubt with strict instructions not to go near the sea. We felt grown-up and independent though that did not prevent us rolling down the dry sand dunes in front of the house, getting the occasional sharp prick from the spiky grass that grew through them.

A walk after tea was part of the ritual, probably over Nannie Moore's Bridge to see if "Brown Willie" was visible. I joined in the chorus of "I can see him" but being short-sighted I never did; I am not sure that I really knew what I was claiming to have seen. Some afternoons a picnic tea was packed and we drove to Crackington Haven in a waggonette pulled by the pair of grey "wedding" horses named Molly and Dolly, or it might be the black "funeral" horses called Butcher Tucker and Freshwater. If our destination was Widemouth Bay the kettle was boiled on the stony beach. My birthday treat was a visit to Hartland Point where the steep hill brought my heart into my mouth as the horses slithered down it. A picnic

September is a Gypsy

September is a gypsy at a jingling country fair,
A gay and laughing maid with scarlet berries in
her hair.
Her lips are crimson blossoms and her hair is
tawny-brown,
And dancing through the bracken goes the russet
of her gown.
So let us go a-walking while the skies are
summer-blue,
For winter's round the corner and the golden
days are few.
We'll store the fleeting sunshine and when days
are short and cold
We shall dance to gypsy music in a dream of
autumn gold.

MARGARET GREENHALGH

tea was abandoned in favour of the tea-shop where to my sorrow saffron cake was offered; I expected an iced birthday cake!

Sunday mornings entailed a walk across the Downs to Poughill church wearing our best clothes. Were we allowed on the shore on Sunday afternoons? I don't remember. Cornwall in the summertime must have had wet, misty periods then as now but memory dictates that they were all golden, shining days and the holidays came to an end all too soon. Then it was back to Waterloo, where a railway omnibus took us to Liverpool Street station, the home terminus for us all. Liverpool Street, with its very special smell and friendly ticket inspectors at the platform barriers . . . CLAIRE McLACHLAN

For What We Are About To Receive

Looking back to a childhood begun over fifty years ago, I was thinking how different our diet was then from that of a modern child. There is a much greater variety of foods today, made possible by improvements in their preservation and packaging, so that out-of-season produce, and that coming from distant lands, is available all the year round.

When I was a small girl breakfasts started with oatmeal porridge, taken from a plain bag and soaked overnight. It had a tendency to be lumpy, and there was no exciting literature on a colourful packet to occupy one's mind when eating it, although when made carefully and smothered in demerara sugar and cream, it was unforgettably good. Bread-and-milk was usual at nursery suppertime; we added salt and pepper to ours and called it "Kiddley Broth", but when away from home we were often given it with sugar, which I found sickly. Packaged cereals were just coming onto the market; one of the first of these was Force which had as its trademark a quaint gentleman with a yellow Nelsonian "queue", called Sunny Jim.

High o'er the fence leaps Sunny Jim,
Force is the food which raises him

must have been the first of advertisement jingles. Beef-tea was a great nursery stand-by, but I remember it as rather tasteless, as was the calf's-foot jelly which was supposed to build us up after illness. It was not until I went to boarding school that I found children were supposed not to like rice-pudding. At home it was cooked slowly, simmering for hours at the back of the kitchen range, until creamy and quite delicious.

The kitchens of childhood memory were mostly vast stone-flagged caverns, hard on a cook's feet when cooking was a day-long business with endless grating, chopping and sieving; everything done the long, hard way, with nothing pre-cooked or prepared for cooking. We had no electrical beaters or blenders, and nothing was ever "instant". Though I must admit that home-cooked ham, "boiled to velvet" as my Mother called it, had much more flavour than the compressed, ready-sliced ham I buy today. I can remember when the first cake-mixes came out, and what fun it was to kneel up at the kitchen table when allowed to cut strips of green angelica and slice the glacé cherries found in the packet, to decorate the fairy cakes in their little paper patties, but I know that housewives felt guilty for using something "easy".

Tinned food was still suspect and had a reputation for being easily contaminated; we had only tinned corned beef and Swiss milk, as we called condensed milk. What a boon is the modern tin-opener — we had only the kind that left a jagged edge after the point was banged in and see-sawed around. As children we ate more bread and less cake and biscuits; if hungry we were sent running with a "jam-butty", a "door-step" with a generous coating of farm butter and home-made jam, but my own children had more sophisticated tastes. If we were thirsty we drank water, cool well-water from a pitcher standing on a slate slab in the back-kitchen, or milk, often warm from the cow. Only on special occasions did we have fizzy ginger beer in a green glass bottle with a fascinating marble on the top. We carried cold tea or herb-beer to the harvest field for the grown-ups, and as a treat were allowed a sip of home-brewed cider from the barrel behind the stable door. We had lots of hot milk and cocoa during cold weather, always with wrinkly "skin" on top, which my school mates used to spoon away with sounds of disgust, but I knew this was the cream coming to the top, because I was used to seeing the shallow pans of milk being scalded on the range, with their risen cream thickening into a deep yellow crust, real Cornish cream.

On the Cornish farm, where I spent much of my childhood, there was always "fry" for breakfast. Delicious sizzling bacon-smells rose to the bedroom to mingle with the apple-scent of fruit laid out for "keeping". Plates of fried home-cured bacon, new-laid eggs, mashed potato, and often left-over cabbage, were followed by slices of bread with marmalade and cream, and buttered "white cake", a not-so-sweet breakfast cake. I suppose we soon ran this down, as I was always ready for a little pasty, hot from the oven, with my initials pricked on its crisp, golden-brown half-moon. It was best eaten held in a strip of brown paper, its warmth comforting to the hand, oozing savoury gravy, while I sat up in an old gnarled apple tree, reading a favourite book.

One delight of my childhood I am sorry my children missed was to nibble my way round the vegetable garden. There were little pods of new peas, small white turnips, bunches of red and black currants, and big yellow gooseberries, skins taut with sweet juice, and there was always keen competition for the white cubes cut from a fresh cabbage stalk when it was being prepared for table. Vile-tasting Gregory powder was waiting for the over-indulgent!

Living in the country meant "butcher's meat" was a treat, only to be had after a visit to the market-town, otherwise we ate our own poultry or wild rabbit, caught with a ferret and nets, or shot in the harvest field as the binder made its way around the last of the standing corn.

Cold rabbit pie, full of tasty jellied meat, ranks with rhubarb or blackberry-and-apple "open" tart, generously dabbed with clotted cream, as a gourmand memory from a time when calories meant nothing.

When a farmer killed a pig, relatives and neighbours were given a portion, so curing sides of bacon and hams hung from the kitchen rafters. Butter-making was done by hand, and there was consternation when in hot sultry weather the butter would not "turn".

"Boughten" bread was rarely seen, and the scent of warming barm and newly-baked loaves are indeed joyous memories. Ice-cream is now prepared under more hygienic conditions, but it does taste so synthetic. Our penny cornets and chase-me-round "shutters" had a real cream flavour, each one individually scooped for us by the Italian vendor underneath the gaily-striped awning of his little cart.

The cheaper kinds of sweets were not wrapped or packeted. The shop-keeper cheerfully weighed out quarters of a pound, or counted out pennyworths of aniseed balls or ogopogo-eyes, a type of miniature gob-stopper which changed colour every few sucks. For a penny one could buy a little sugared birdcage, complete with bird inside, or a slab of honeycomb toffee we called "Peggy's leg", liquorice "boot-laces", or "black-jack", a hard black glossy toffee, almost unbitable. There was a shop at Deal which sold humbugs in every size and flavour, while our village shop specialised in "fishes", boiled sweets in many-coloured fishy shapes, served in a small funnel of paper, folded with a flourish and presented to outstretched little fingers as a veritable horn of plenty.

We were kept busy gathering the spoils of hillside and hedgerow for use in the kitchen; mushrooms picked at dawn from dew-drenched sheep pastures; frothy elderflowers and sunny dandelions for wine; acrid sloes for "gin" blackberries and whortleberries (hurts, we called them) for tarts and jam, tiny wild strawberries to eat with clotted cream, and hazelnuts, each in their season. We nipped off the tender shoots of hawthorn, our "bread-and-cheese", as we walked the springtime lanes, and enjoyed the tart taste of sorrel growing in the meadows, then later in the year there were mallow seeds and beech mast to chew.

The average child has a much better and more varied diet today, and statistics show that children are taller and heavier than their counterparts of fifty years ago, when the words "vitamin" and "protein" were unknown in a housewife's vocabulary. All the same, as country children we did pretty well, even if we had tangerines only at Christmas-time.

And we have such a wonderful hoard of memories to feast on . . .

DOREEN BARFIELD

THE EMPTY POCKET

A Childhood Memory

In my pocket nestles my chestnut conker, shiny brown and strongly firm. The air is sweetly cool with a peaty fragrance, the autumn sun warms only lightly with quickening speed as its greater self is in other climes. I turn to see Tom's unsteady approach, crutches walking him urgently into the glade; his expression lightens up on seeing me and he tells me that he is determined to find the king of all conkers and would I join in the search. I agree gladly, grateful to put off the moment for leaving this enchanted place. After a while I realise with slowing energy that no conker left to be found can be measured up to mine. A robin flits about us and faintly a wood pigeon calls his rhyme; I notice the sudden wearying of Tom's patient frame and his eyes hold resigned disappointment as he remarks that it is time to return home. He turns awkwardly round, only to be jerked back at my cry of delight as I bend swiftly to feel among the damping leaves and then rise, holding in my hand the very conker that he had been hoping to find. I hand it over to his almost reverent grasp and again our eyes meet; his now glow with sheer delight... and mine with bright pretence. As we go our slow way home my hand finds strange comfort in an empty pocket.

JOAN PRIMROSE WELLS

Our Medicine Cupboard

During the 1920s, before most drugs and penicillin had been discovered, people had to rely on simpler remedies. In the country many of these were home-made and no housewife worth her salt would have been found without a well-stocked medicine cupboard and a variety of medicinal plants in her garden.

I well remember such a cupboard in my childhood home; the glass doors were covered with a patterned translucent paper, which gave them a stained-glass effect. Inside were all kinds of bottles, jars and tins all ready to hand for any emergency, for in the depths of the country the chemist's shop was too far distant.

At the first sign of a sniffle or a sneeze we children were sent to school with our handkerchiefs liberally sprinkled with eucalyptus oil, and if we complained of a sore throat we had to wear a silk scarf as protection against the cold, for many of us had a long walk to school. Some children wore one of their mother's black cashmere stockings round their throat, with a hot boiled potato wrapped in it! Others had a "collop" of bacon round the throat, held in place with a piece of silk.

Father had several pet remedies for a sore throat and used to ring the changes if his throat did not improve with the first treatment. Beginning with equal parts of vinegar and glycerine stirred in a cup, or rather several cups placed about the house so that he could take a spoonful when he passed, he would go on to onions sliced thinly in an earthenware dish and placed on the hob in front of the fire to cook slowly. No electric cookers in those days. Other favourite cure-alls were butter and sugar worked together, and honey and lemon. Of course he was a firm believer in gargling with something particularly nasty tasting.

Little sister had a delicate constitution and only needed to cough twice to be encased in a brown paper waistcoat worn next to the skin. This garment was well pricked all over with a large needle to make air holes so that circulation of the air to the body was not interfered with. Before it was put on, it was well smeared with goose grease (made by rendering the leaf of fat from the Christmas goose); she often wore this for weeks as her coughs were long lasting. Every time she had a bath it was taken off and more goose grease applied; some would also be rubbed on her chest and back. As her cough improved the waistcoat was reduced by tearing a little piece off daily until it was little more than a collar.

If our colds worsened despite the eucalyptus, silk scarves, hot potatoes etc, we were given a hot mustard bath and put to bed with a drink of hot milk well laced with treacle, ginger, or mustard — or a cup of blackcurrant tea, all to get "a good sweat on".

To ease a stuffed-up nose, goose grease or Vaseline was rubbed inside and outside our noses. I didn't much care for the goose grease on my chest but positively hated camphorated oil to which we sometimes had to resort when the goose grease ran out.

For "tummy pains" we were given ginger in water, horrific to swallow — your mouth and throat seemed to be on fire. The trick was to keep the mouth shut for several minutes after taking it, until the burning sensation subsided somewhat. Indian brandy and Indian bark were two other remedies which were less unpleasant to take and for this reason were not considered to be as effective, because for some unknown reason, it was commonly believed that the nastier the medicine the surer the cure. Meadowsweet flowers and camomile flowers made into tea were widely used for stomach disorders.

To keep us in rude health during the winter, spoonfuls of cod-liver oil emulsion or cod-liver oil and malt were thrust down our protesting throats and foods warranted to keep the cold out were offered to us before we left on our long walk to school. We were pressed to eat up our good oatmeal porridge and not to leave our fried bacon, egg and fried bread. Our bedtime meal was often "pobs" — bread and milk — to make us sleep, they said.

Soon after the first daffodils were out and the hedges were beginning to turn green we were dosed with sulphur and treacle (brimstone and treacle) "to clear the blood" and had periodically to drink senna pod tea to give "a good clean out".

For cuts, wounds, and scratches, zinc ointment was used in the first instance, but if it took bad ways and needed "drawing" they used boracic ointment — or boracic and pink lint wrung out of hot water, covered with a piece of green oiled silk and cotton wool. Or a poultice of bran or bread was applied; later kaolin poultice appeared on the scene.

Some more primitive methods were the use of an ivy leaf for cuts, right side down to heal and wrong side to draw, cinder tea for infant indigestion, and the application of a cobweb to a bad wound to staunch bleeding. This was an old farming remedy used when a cow came up from the field with a sloughed horn, but which some applied to humans — most unhygienic.

Those days have gone and we have drugs for every ailment, yet how often do we see our modern children easing a nettle sting by rubbing it with a dock leaf and saying "Nettle go out and dock go in"?

HAZEL COTTAM

Gold and Silver Memories

Memories of childhood
Flit across my mind,
I catch the gold and silver ones
And leave the rest behind;
Swinging in the garden,
Apples on the ground,
Tadpoles in the little pond
And beauty all around.

Someone with a heart of gold
Sitting by my bed,
Wiping very tenderly
My tear-stained eyes so red;
For when the village church bells
Began their ding-dong-dell
A child would sob most piteously
Lest "Puss was in the Well".

Fishing with a home-made rod,
Just longing for a trout.
Nearly fell into the stream
When I pulled one out!
Memories of childhood
Dance into my brain,
I catch the gold and silver ones
And live them once again.

CICELY SMITH

THE STORE-CUPBOARD

To many people nowadays "the store cupboard" means the rather ungetatable top shelf in the kitchen where a few tinned or dried foods are kept for an emergency. Fifty years ago the store cupboard was a very different matter. It was either a small room, or it was one or two large cupboards *not* in the kitchen, but whichever it was, it was kept locked and only the mistress of the house had the key. Now that houses and families are generally smaller, and most foods are pre-packed, the ordinary family does not so often buy in bulk and have a regular delivery from the grocer; instead the housewife collects small quantities from the supermarket three or four times a week. Also, now that the mistress of the house and the cook are usually one and the same person, the necessity for a locked cupboard has gone, and so has the daily ritual of issuing stores.

Every day after breakfast there was a conference between my mother and the cook about the food for the day, and then if stores were required my mother would go to the store cupboard — in our case two very large, deep cupboards upstairs — followed by a maid carrying a tray of containers for refilling. Large white jars with blue lettering on them would be filled with flour, sugar and rice, but there were also stores of more interest to watching children, such as sultanas or glacé cherries, and with luck a few of these might find their way into a hopeful, waiting hand. The containers would be filled from thick blue or brown paper bags containing seven or fourteen pounds of the commodity.

When the bulk goods arrived from the grocer, there was the ceremony of checking the list and putting everything away — again with the possibility of a little youthful sampling.

On the floor of the store cupboard, though it might be kept in the larder, would be a huge earthenware crock containing preserved eggs, "put down" in the spring when eggs came down in price to 8d or 9d per dozen, that is, under 4p in modern currency. These preserved eggs would be used for all cakes and puddings during the late summer and winter when the price of eggs went up. A number of smaller crocks would contain salted runner beans, either home grown or bought very cheaply when the supply was at its peak. There was no freezing of vegetables then, and if there was a glut it was good for the housewife and just too bad for the grower!

Once a year the whole house would reek of hot marmalade, and the next day trays of jars would be brought upstairs to be labelled, dated and put away. A similar procedure would take place with various jams in season, and on a high shelf would be rows of Kilner jars containing fruit preserved in syrup, pears from the garden and plums bought in quantity at the height of their short season.

In another part of the room, or in our case in another deep cupboard, would be the stores that must be kept away from food, i.e. soap and cleaning materials. On the floor there was a criss-cross tower, such as a child might build with long wooden bricks, made of bars of yellow soap, stored in that way so that it would dry out. Beside it was a wire with two wooden handles used for cutting the bars into "pieces". This yellow soap, the smell of which always revolted me, was used for all household washing and cleaning.

Nearby would be a large crate or cardboard box containing tablets of plain, cream-coloured toilet soap, probably bought in bulk at a reduced price as "bruised". Tablets were not individually wrapped and elaborately packed as they are now, and the cakes of soap were much more likely to get knocked about, but "bruised" soap was just as efficient for scrubbing dirty knees and as no-one wore jeans then our knees required frequent scrubbing.

Now that a built-in kitchen cupboard contains all household necessities, pre-packed in convenient small quantities and stored in the room in which they will be used, life is no doubt much more convenient . . . but somehow a little duller.

PEGGY WINCKWORTH

Our Diamond Day

It's sixty years of married life
But that's not the way to score —
For years are made of weeks and days
With all the days before.

Twenty-one thousand to begin,
With one hundred and fifteen more
For life was lived by days alone
And now all are in store.

The happy day remembered yet
In spite of war's alarms
When hand-in-hand you took the road
That still has many charms.

The days were filled with thankfulness
For mercies great and small —
For families, friends, and sorrows too,
Each day embraced them all.

The silver and golden years are passed
Today the diamond shines
But not as bright or crystal clear
As the love you have enshrined.

For God is good. Each day He provides
The strength to walk the way —
Walk on, dear friends, the path that leads
Unto that perfect day . . .

GEORGE PEARSON

Our Village FLOWER SHOW

One of the exciting events in our village was the annual Flower Show, always held on the last Thursday in July. I suppose there must have been occasions when the day was cloudy or even wet. If there were, I can't remember them. My recollection is that on the day of the Flower Show the sun always shone from a cloudless blue sky.

The chief interest for us youngsters was the showing of wild flowers and grasses. An entrance fee of 3d was charged. For this, one not only gained admission to the show but it was possible to win money prizes; as much as two shillings (10p) as a first prize, untold wealth in the early days of the century. After a year or two of competing I discovered the trick of winning prizes, namely to collect a wide variety of flowers and grasses, and particularly flowers of bright colours.

Poppies were important (and were then plentiful), but these had to be gathered on the morning of the show, otherwise they drooped and died before the exhibit could be judged. As one who well knew the woods and countryside I had no difficulty in finding some of the rarer wild flowers and grasses. As I carefully arranged the exhibit in a 2lb jam jar I had visions of the prize I felt sure would be mine, especially when I gleefully saw the drooping poppies of the other hopeful but inexperienced youngsters.

At half past two in the afternoon we followed the village brass band to the grounds of "The Hall" where the Flower Show was held. The Hall itself was a massive

Victorian mansion owned by a man who had been lucky enough to find diamonds in South Africa. That he was a man of untold wealth was evidenced by the fact that he owned a car, then the only one in the village. So after we had followed the band to the Hall grounds, we gazed in awe at the large mansion and wondered why one small man and his even smaller wife could possibly want so many rooms and such an army of servants.

If diamonds are a girl's best friend, they also proved a friend to the villagers, for on the occasion of the Flower Show the grounds were made available to all and the extensive greenhouses were open to view — and how the ripening grapes and peaches made our mouths water! Our chief interest, however, was the flower marquee, to which we made a dash to see who had carried off the valuable prizes. I usually won a first or second prize, and to me two bob were then riches indeed.

Another thrill was a competition, open to women only, to catch and hold a pig with a well-greased tail. The lady who could hold the pig could claim it and take it home to fatten for Christmas. As the pig squealed in fright, we squealed in delight as one after another of the village women in their long skirts grabbed the pig's tail, immediately to see the poor animal escape her grasp. There was, of course, an art in holding a pig with a greasy tail. It was to wait until a dozen or more of the competitors had grasped the tail, for by then much of the grease had come off — on the ladies' hands. Choosing the psychological moment, the lady who held on long enough to claim the pig would surreptitiously thrust the handkerchief she had been holding (to keep her hands dry) into a pocket, make a quick grab (for the pig was then getting tired) and as the animal escaped from the right hand, grab it quickly again with the left.

The pig was always won by one of the two or three women who had mastered this technique. It was even suggested that the handkerchief of the winner had been

well sprinkled with sand! The less experienced had succeeded only in tiring themselves and getting their hands covered with grease. The lady who triumphantly carried off the pig was as fresh as a daisy and her hands scarcely needed washing.

Another feature was the Baby Show — and certainly the event wouldn't have been complete without it. True, many of the babies more resembled pumpkins than flowers, for it was the fat ones who won the prizes, which were donated by one of the Ladies Bountiful. She was a large, well-fed female who tipped the scales at 16 stone or more. I forget her real name. We rude boys called her "Mrs. Jumbo", and she was always asked to judge the Baby Show. Naturally she chose the fat ones as the winners. So, weeks before the Flower Show mothers began the process of fattening their offspring. Toddlers were filled with milk, meat pie and puddings until they looked like miniature Samsons. It was probably not an economic exercise, for the top prize money amounted to only five shillings (25p). But then, fattening pigs was probably not an economic proposition either, yet many of the villagers kept a pig. And it was regarded as a greater credit to produce a fat baby than a fat pig!

The mothers whose offspring had won prizes were delighted. The rest were jealous — even furious, thinking of all the food that had gone into the effort. As the number of disappointed customers exceeded the satisfied ones, the Baby Show didn't add to the harmony of the village.

In the evening of the Flower Show there was dancing on the lawn, accompanied by the village brass band. So a wonderful day came to an end.

On the last Thursday in July 1914 (I was then aged 15) I walked home from the Flower Show on a perfect summer evening, and an older boy said: "It looks as though there may be a war." That was the first time I had heard of any threat of war. Just over a week later Britain *was* at war.

Many of the village young men who that afternoon had taken part in the races and competitions were soon to be fighting in France and Gallipoli. Many never came back. Their names are inscribed on the war memorial in the churchyard.

The 1914 Flower Show was the last to be held in our village. The end of an era had come. The fun was over, for it was the last event of our settled world.

JOHN DUNFORD

RAILWAY CHILDREN

Everyone called us the railway children but, like E.K. Nesbit's family, we belonged to the railway only by adoption. We were born in York. Suddenly one morning we woke to find ourselves in beautiful but completely strange countryside. Today, it seems that those years we spent as children at Levisham Station, where the line to Whitby cuts through the hollow of Newton Dale, occurred at a particularly peaceful time. We were too young to know how wrong we were!

It was 1943. Almost every night enemy bombers droned over our home in York. Then Hitler turned his attention to cathedral cities and it was our turn. The old wooden Guildhall blazed. Stones from St. Mary's Abbey opposite our house flew across the road and chipped pieces from our brick shelter. After an especially sickening whine, pause, thud, I remember my mother remarking, "That's our house." It was.

Next morning, as she made what breakfast she could for us in the ruins of her kitchen, she told us we were going with our neighbours to share their cottage at Lockton. She explained that this was a tiny village, perched on a hill-top on the edge of the Whitby moors. I found my needlework box with all my treasures inside it, and my brother his Meccano, and we set off through the smoking streets for the station. Most of the front of the building had vanished into a heap of rubble but some trains were still running. We squeezed into a troop train going north, packed with soldiers on a few days' leave.

All the seats, gangways and corridors were crammed with weary men in khaki. One young soldier slept all the way to Pickering with his head on Mother's knee! From Pickering, it was only a few miles to Lockton.

Then we heard that there was a plate-layer's cottage standing empty a mile or so away at Levisham Station. We could move in. Again we gathered our treasures and walked along the valley to our new home. The cottage stood close by the line, dwarfed by steep wooded hillsides crowned with great sweeps of moorland. There was a signal box, a waiting room, a bigger house labelled "Station Master", and that was all — no sign of a village. We loved the cottage right from the start. The front door led straight into a stone-flagged kitchen with a huge fireplace piled with logs. Over it swung a heavy iron reckon with adjustable hooks. From these Mother hung cooking pots like miniature witches' cauldrons. But out of these she produced magical meals. She baked in a battered, creaking side oven, but I can still remember those Yorkshire puddings, so crisp and light they seemed to float out of their tins! From the kitchen, one door led into the neat front parlour, and another opened to reveal a flight of stairs leading to the two bedrooms. They were equipped with bedsteads with shiny brass rails and feather mattresses, and washstands with blue china jugs and bowls. Gleaming brass oil lamps hung from hooks in the ceilings, mingling their sharper smell with the wood smoke and the scent of wild flowers crowded into the deep recesses of the windows.

Outside was even better. A path ran from the back door of the cottage across the yard, then over a field to a stream half buried in wild raspberry bushes. This was our favourite playground. But we had a problem. The field was the jealously guarded home of an old, very bad-tempered goat. He loathed us, but for some reason he became Mother's devoted admirer. He followed her about the field, chewing clothes pegs as she hung out the washing.

Our station served two village communities: Levisham, tucked away out of sight behind one hill-top, and Newton, equally invisible behind another. Jack was the king-pin holding us all together. He worked the signals, checked mail, issued tickets and saw the trains through safely. He always knew whom to expect for any train and whether a slight delay might be necessary for would-be passengers still struggling down the hillside. We loved to perch in his signal box behind its row of fascinating levers and watch the trains roar past. Not many stopped — most tore by, clanking and hissing steam, sparks flying from their shining wheels. Most dragged long processions of wagons with mysteriously-shaped tarpaulin covers blowing back occasionally to reveal a gun muzzle or a glimpse of a tank. We waved to the few passenger trains so often crowded with men in uniform. But in spite of these reminders, to us in our sleepy valley the war seemed very far away.

Overnight, everything changed. The Army began manoeuvres in Newton Dale and we found ourselves in the middle of a battlefield! The quiet hillsides crackled with gunfire, tanks rumbled along the cart tracks, and tempting rope bridges were slung across our stream. Long rows of stooping figures filed along the skyline. We delighted in all this. (Looking back now, I don't think it ever occurred to us there might be any danger.) From the tops of our favourite climbing trees, we watched detachments of soldiers tracking each other across the valley, always ready to supply them with more or less reliable directions! A thick hedge divided the field behind our cottage from a cart track leading to the stream. We decided this hedge had tremendous strategic importance. It was lined by successive waves of soldiers, lying on their stomachs with their rifles sticking through the branches. They produced tin mugs and we went up and down the line with pots of tea. A sharp watch was kept, and at the cry "Sarge!" the tin mugs disappeared and we

had to dive out of sight into the hedge, teapots and all!

One day we waved to a train full of soldiers who looked different. Their uniforms were a shade of light blue we had never seen before. When they saw us an avalanche of chocolate bars came flying out of the carriage windows. We feasted for weeks on this American generosity!

Our English Isle

Dear people of our English Isle,
In us, let kindliness prevail.
No apartheid, or hate, or spite;
Or worldly men who twist their might.
They view no beauty of the moon,
No silver dew on morning lawns.
See far therefore, and think upon
Those lit and lovely lawns of light
Beyond the view of present sight.
Remember, too, this briefest night
In which our souls do not delight
Is but the prelude, short and sharp,
To Love's true heaven of the heart.

ESME VERNON

The only time our little station was really busy was Thursday, when everyone from both villages and the scattered cottages along the line-side went to Pickering market. This was our day out, too. We caught the early-morning milk train which was always sure to run and offered reduced fares. After the quiet of our valley we delighted in the bustle of the market, the animals in their stalls and the friendly shops. The highlight was a bought tea. In a small café at the foot of the steps to the church we ate curd tarts and muffins spread with rich yellow butter. And after tea we went to the Pictures. Did it matter if sometimes the projector broke down in such a happy place where everyone joked and chatted to all-comers? We always had to leave early to catch the last train home so we never discovered how the films ended anyway. We finished them to suit ourselves!

Levisham station was our home for two years. We walked miles beside the lines which ran like gleaming silver ribbons along the valley, picking wild strawberries, gathering armfuls of red willow herb and admiring the snakes which lay curled up sleeping among the warm stones. We harvested raspberries, blackberries and bilberries from the high moors above the valley. Every day we went "wooding", making our own stack among the trees not far from home. There were the mysterious remains of old iron workings to explore and a Roman road to discover, forging its precise way over Stoney Moor to Goathland.

Some years ago I went back to Levisham station. I found it deserted and ruined. But that is not the end of the story. I find that now part of the line has been re-opened and the station restored by the North Yorkshire Moors Historical Railways Trust. Steam trains whistle once more through Newton Dale.

ANNE MARIE EDWARDS

HALLELUJAH!
...and Salmon Sandwiches

When I was a little girl Good Friday was my favourite day of the year. It brought "The Outing" to Farndon Chapel for tea and service. For me Good Friday always began on Thursday night, with the "getting ready" for the big day. After tea my mother would put the kettle and a saucepan full of water to heat in readiness for my "real good wash".

I remember standing on the prickly coco-matting in the back kitchen in my liberty bodice and bloomers. The hot water would be poured out of the kettle into the chipped, white enamel bowl. My mother would then proceed to "soap the flannel"; the flannel being a piece of my father's interlock pants. It always amazed me how my mother knew the difference between flannel and dishcloth as the same garment supplied both. Sometimes there was proper toilet soap but more often than not it would be a half-a-pound section of Lifebuoy from the scrubbing bucket. This meant that bits of grit together with chippings from the bottom of the enamel bowl would cling to the flannel and be vigorously rubbed onto my face. If I protested my mother would say "Oh get along with you" and give me an extra rub.

Now a *real* good wash was very different from a good wash. After the first general onslaught on my face, my mother would start to specialise; wrapping the flannel around her first finger she would attack my ears, poking, prodding and twisting. I still recall the terrible swishing noise it made. After the final once-over I was told to "Hang over the bowl" to be rinsed or I would look as if I had been "washed in pea soup." It's a wonder I didn't for

by now she had worked up such a lather that it was a very suddy rinse. Next came hands and arms. Now a good wash stopped at the elbows but a *real* good wash not only took in elbows and armpits but shoulders as well.

The stopper was then put in the sink and the contents of the bowl poured in. To this was added the saucepanful of hot water. I was then lifted up to stand in it. I had been "topped", now, bloomers removed, I had to be tailed. If I wasn't washed properly all over, "I would have the dogs after me." Anyway that was what my mother said and, as I was very frightened of dogs, I bore this without a murmur.

Then came knees and at this stage "battle really commenced." My knees were never free of sores, grazes or scabs. Should one of the scabs be half-hanging free my mother's business-like expression, plus the gritty flannel, would fill me with alarm. I would cup my hands over my knees to protect them; "mind your hands" my mother would say. This request being ignored, they would be forcibly removed. Again I would cup them over. This was repeated a few times; then she would lose patience and administer a sharp slap. If you have ever experienced a sharp slap with a wet hand, you will realise "sharp" is the right word. Carefully she would wash round the sores and gently dab them dry. The operation completed mother would say "there now what did I tell you, it didn't hurt a bit did it?"

I had to admit it didn't — it never did — but we always had a battle. Everything from top to bottom had to be clean on for "The Outing". "In case of accidents," my mother would say, and that she would die of shame if anyone belonging to her was taken to hospital and found to be in need of a "good fetling".

After my "good fetling" I would run into the living-room where my clean Magyar-style nightdress, made out of a remnant from the market, would be having a final air and warm.

I stood on the home-made navy and red rag rug to be brushed and combed. My straight, shoulder-length, mousy hair would be twisted and tortured by rags. Sometimes I would cry "too tight, too tight" only to be told that "Pride must bear a pinch." Now bed. No books this night. Straight to sleep. I had a long day in front of me and had to be up early. Looking back I can't think why because "The Outing" did not start until two o'clock, but I never questioned it then.

And now, the "big day", Friday morning and the first wonderful event: breakfast of Hot Cross Buns and hot sweet tea with my father, then into the front room we would go. I would listen to my father practise hymns and voluntary on the organ, for the Sunday Services. After a while he would strike up some lively tunes and we would sing together.

This racket brought in my mother telling us to "Hold your noise! It's like bedlam let loose!" At this my father would grab her round the not-too-slender waist, waltz her round and round and out through the back door, all the while ignoring her request to "Give over do," and not to be so soft. She would speak sharply, go very red and pretend not to like it. I would follow, joining in the fun. He would let her go, only to give her bottom a slap as she turned away. At this I would hold my breath, thinking how dare he take such a liberty, but she would only smile at him. He would then reach for his pipe and settle down for a "bit of a read". I would go out to play after being cautioned "not to get dirty, or go out of the street and to remember I had my clean underthings on and my best shoes, and to keep away from "that Katy Smithers." I couldn't understand why, as she was always more fun than anyone else. I liked her the best . . . and all the boys did too!

After this, the leisurely pace of the morning increased in tempo to a frenzied rush. My mother would suddenly jump to her feet saying she couldn't sit there all day, she couldn't just begin to get herself ready, she'd got the table to clear, pots to wash, fire to bank down and me to get ready. No, she'd never do it. She'd never be ready in time, we would just have to go without her, that's all.

We never did go without her, she was always ready. But we always had that performance whenever we went anywhere.

At last we were ready for off. There would be a consultation on the door-step. Was the back door locked, the gas-taps turned off, the fireguard in place and the windows fastened? We were only going to be away for a few hours in the next village but we might have been going to the ends of the earth.

The meeting place for "The Outing" was outside the chapel gates. I can see them all now. My Grandma with her big fur muff with the long silky tails discarded only for a few weeks in the middle of summer. In it as well as her hands would be her hymn-book and a few cough sweets wrapped in tissue-paper. Various uncles and aunts would be there, including my favourites, Aunt Amy and Uncle Fred. There would be Aunt Fanny, 4ft 11ins, with her life-long friend Miss Fox, 6ft at least, or so she seemed to me then; Mr. and Mrs. Vasey, and Edna and Mr. and Mrs. Pollard. Mrs. Pollard always had one eye full of tears that she was continually wiping. I thought her so clever to cry with one eye. She confused me because she cried even when she laughed. I often tried to do it but with no success. There were Mr. and Mrs. Hall. Mrs. Hall always referred to her husband as "Ooer Herbert" instead of Our Herbert. On asking why I was told because she came from Hull. Not a very satisfactory explanation to me. She also cleaned the chapel and had the keys. I thought she was rich and owned the place.

Whilst everyone was looking for the late-comers the waggonette would come dashing round the opposite end of the street. I always saw it first. I wasn't looking for Mr. and Mrs. Blythe, especially Sylvia . . . always the last to arrive. Sylvia was the exact opposite to Katy Smithers. She was a paragon of all the virtues and was held as a pattern for me to follow.

The horses drew up alongside the curb. The driver got down and fixed the steps at the rear of the waggonette. The ladies and children were then helped in, followed by the men who would sort out and sit next to their respective spouses. Away we would go, sitting in two long rows facing each other on seats that went the full length of the waggonette. I would make an attempt to kneel on the seat, only to be told to "sit down ladylike . . . like Sylvia".

As we jogged along we passed the more energetic members of the chapel who had decided to walk. These were the Band of Hope and the Christian Endeavour, some walking in groups, others straggling behind in twos — the courting couples. The ladies waved and the men raised their hats as we passed them, but from Uncle Fred the courting couples would get a nod, a grin and a wink that said an awful lot.

At last we turned off the main road into the village. The waggonette would draw up outside the little chapel whose members were on the steps to give welcome. We would be greeted like long-lost cousins. There was hand shaking, back-patting, ladies kissing, everyone asking after the others' welfare.

When the greetings were over we went on "The Walk" down to the river. Some of our ladies would stay behind to help prepare the tea and "Oh Happy Day" when my mother was one of them. She would read me the riot act . . . Yes, I could go with the others as long as I didn't get dirty, didn't go too near the water's edge, minded my Ps and Qs and kept hold of my father's hand. I would promise all this and away we would go. Soon my father would be talking music with the village organist and I would let go his hand and be off. I knew a short cut to the "turning back point". This enabled me to have a few minutes' play on the "clapper gates".

I always *meant* to keep clean but somehow never managed it. One year in particular was disastrous. I found a "Cowslip Pancake". It looked hard and sun-baked. I put my foot over it, then on it, very lightly. I don't know how it happened, but my foot disappeared. It wasn't hard at all. The crusty top had deceived me. I remember going down to the water's edge, wetting a clump of grass and trying to clean myself. I thought I didn't look too bad when I caught up with my father again, slipping my hand into his. I don't think he had ever missed me because he looked so surprised when my mother rounded on him for my filthy state on our return. He looked at me, turned to my mother with a bewildered look saying "But we haven't been near any mud"; neither of them realised that it wasn't mud. This exasperated her. "Don't talk so soft.

You must have done. It's always the same. Work my fingers to the bone. Try my best but the more I do the more I may do. Look at her mouth, if I've told you once I've told you a dozen times not to give her those mucky Meloids." Poor Father, he never knew that when he was absent-mindedly handing round the tin I would take as many as I could, manoeuvre them onto my teeth and pretend I'd had them all knocked out.

Yanking me to her, my mother would then begin the "mopping up operation". This was done by spitting on her handkerchief and vigorously rubbing it over my face. I wouldn't have minded so much if I could have used my own spit but I didn't dare suggest it.

The next highlight of the day was the "Tea" which was held in the village schoolroom. We would make our way slowly, because it was unseemly to appear to be too eager to eat (so Aunt Fanny said when on one occasion I got there first).

There would be two long tables, each covered with a snowy cloth. Cups, saucers and plates would border the tables, and down the centre were plates of bread and butter, brown and white balm loaf, fruit cake and, best of all, salmon sandwiches. I looked forward to having them from one year to the next, for we never had anything as grand as salmon at home.

Before tea began we all sang "*Be present at our table, Lord,*" and then sat. This was the cue for the helpers to go into action. They were the village ladies in their best dresses which were protected by little white muslin aprons. They would fill up the teacups from the copper urns that graced both ends of the table. Just as I thought the cups would run over they would turn the tap and disaster would be averted. They would flit and hover in the background watching for empty cups and replenishing plates.

Tea over and the proper note sounded, we sang "*Thy creatures bless and grant that we may feast in Paradise with thee.*" Paradise to me then was the promise of an everlasting feast with God on salmon sandwiches. After tea came the service in Farndon Chapel. I remember one year that brought me the biggest walloping I ever had.

Among the worshippers was old Mr. Beckitt. He had been a faithful and fervent worshipper all his life and the older he got the more fervour he found. I looked forward to hearing Mr. Beckitt. He would listen to the preacher for a few minutes then give a mumbled "*Hear, hear*". From this he would work himself up to a noisy climax. His performance always made me giggle but my mother's restraining hand on my knee kept me within bounds. The preacher droned on and Mr. Beckitt was having a "rather-longer-than-usual" quiet time when suddenly he leapt to his feet shouting. "*Praise the Lord, Praise the Lord.*" Mr. Pollard, sitting in the pew in front having forty winks, also leapt to his feet with shock at being woken up so suddenly. He quickly recovered himself and sat down. This turned my giggling into hearty laughter and I couldn't stop. Even the severe poke between my shoulders from Grandma sitting behind had no effect.

Mr. Beckitt by this time had really got going. He was having more to say than the preacher and was in better voice, too. The more he shouted the more hysterical I got. I rocked backwards and forwards, my heels banging on the under-part of the seat, but on seeing the expression

THE SAMPLER

Among the attic's junk a rag I find,
crumpled and soiled, into the rubbish flung:
now, I remove with shuddering touch, but kind,
the sampler Grandma worked when very young.
A cottage vaguely seen, its stitches frayed;
the wool in drabbest grey, the colours blurred,
her name in full, embroidered: "wrought" it said
when ten years old, then her address. Memory stirred
through childhood days, when I had gazed with awe
at this same sampler, framed above her bed;
its colours bright, the linen white. I saw
her as a child, my Grandma, long since dead.
I'll have it cleaned: hung on my bedroom-wall,
we'll feel her love outpouring to us all.

DORIS SEYS PRYCE

on my mother's face I tried to stop. By this time Mr. Beckitt was up on his feet with outstretched arms and looking towards Heaven was shouting "*Hallelujah, Hallelujah*". I must have gone mad because I yelled "*Hallelujah*" after him! There was a dreadful silence. My "*Hallelujah*" seemed to have stunned everyone.

A high-pitched giggle from Sylvia broke the silence and the next thing I knew I was being marched down the aisle. The door firmly shut behind us, my mother proceeded to "give me what I had been asking for, for a long time". Her hand went up and down onto the target, only stopping to give me a good shake. My hat fell off, so did hers. I tried to get past her but though she was only five feet tall she weighed twelve stone. At last she stopped, I think from sheer exhaustion, turned to go back into the chapel, changed her mind and stepped back onto my foot. I let out a piercing yell which brought my father and grandmother out with a rush.

The preacher brought the service to an early close, and we climbed back into the waggonette. Between sobs I could hear my mother saying "To think that a child of mine . . . Never been so ashamed in my life . . . Last time I shall bring her." This last remark really upset me and I began blubbering again. No more waggonette, no more Mr. Beckitt, no more salmon sandwiches. I remember my father passing me his handkerchief and my mother snatching it back and throwing it at him angrily, ordering him to "leave the little madam alone." Then she sat and stared stonily to the front, ignoring me.

On the opposite side of the waggonette sat Sylvia in all her splendour, as tidy and neat as when we started out. She sat staring at me. I knew how I looked. Red blotchy face, swollen eyes, hair ribbon hanging on the last quarter-inch of straggly ringlet. One sock had wriggled itself down into my dirty shoe and the button had come off the other one and it was flapping half off my foot. Suddenly Sylvia leaned forward and said "You are a bad girl and you made me misbehave too." My arm shot out and with the flat of my hand I pushed her face back. The sudden push jerked her hat off and over the side of the waggonette it went. My father got out to find it. He fished it out of the dyke, boarded the waggonette and rammed it down over Sylvia's eyes. It had lost its perfection; besides being muddy, it now had a slit round the top of the crown and, as we jogged along, like my shoe it flapped.

Mrs. Blythe said I was a "little heathen" and she

didn't know what the end of me would be. Then, something about me being a bad influence. At this my mother came to life again. *She* could call me that, but woe betide anyone else who did. Remarks passed between them, making them very angry, but I was too tired to listen.

At last we were put down at the top of our street. I fully realised my disgrace when, instead of the three of us walking hand in hand, I was pushed in front to walk alone. We walked in silence. In silence a cup of milk was handed to me. In silence I was marched up to bed. My mother, through tight lips, hoped I was pleased with my day's work. She turned out the light and left me.

All next day no one spoke to me. Mother didn't want to and father daren't. I was banished to the front room with a book about missionaries. Sunday came. I went to chapel. I wasn't allowed to sit with my best friend, Ruby Coyne.

That was punishment enough, but Sylvia sat there. I did notice she had her weekday hat on, but I was really too miserable to get much satisfaction out of that.

This silent treatment was worse than the Good Friday hiding. I went home to sit with the "Missionaries" again although I had read it twice. Mother called me into the kitchen for tea but there was no plate set for me. Then with a grim look my mother banged one down, saying "There, though you don't deserve them."

It was a plate of salmon sandwiches. I knew at last that I was forgiven.

By the next year Mr. Beckitt had died, my father had "got on" and salmon was part of our usual diet. But Good Friday was never the same again.

W.M. HOPEWELL

Hidden Treasures

I am growing older
And wondering what to do
With all my hidden treasures
Before I say "adieu".
For years they've all been locked away
In cupboards dark and cold,
Lovely Dresden china,
Silver, glass, and gold.

I know that many precious things
Must be locked away
But if they are your very own
Enjoy them while you may.
I opened wide my cupboards
And took my treasures out,
Polished them and dusted
And put them all about.

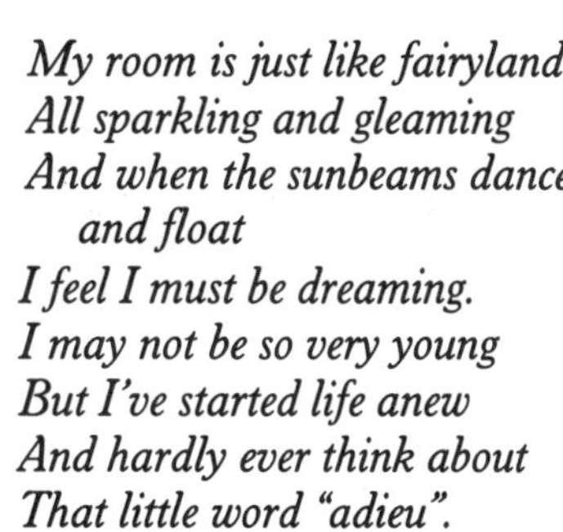

My room is just like fairyland
All sparkling and gleaming
And when the sunbeams dance
and float
I feel I must be dreaming.
I may not be so very young
But I've started life anew
And hardly ever think about
That little word "adieu".

CICELY SMITH

Mushroom Magic

In the greengrocer's window they were dingy amongst the riotous colours of the shining apples and tomatoes, the flamboyant oranges and velvet peaches. They looked machine-made in their uniformity of size, their bruised gills brown and lustreless. They were not real mushrooms, I concluded, and regarding them I found my mind going back over the years to girlhood days lived under the enchantment of the countryside, and to the magic of mushrooming.

In those days mushrooms appeared only briefly in the shops in their true season, when they grew in their true habitat, the green depth of grass heavy with September dew, warmed by autumn's mellow sun. Their growing places being far-flung and few, they were highly prized, the villagers finding an eager and profitable market for them. Competition in their culling was so intense that the entire local community annually took on a temporary guise of adversaries.

In consequence my school-friend Maggie and I

employed our considerable innate cunning in concealing every minute detail of our own expeditions, never betraying by as much as a word either the time or direction of operation, and setting off while the rest of the world still slept.

To us mushrooming was almost an art, a kind of cult which we practised with a peculiar jumble of knowledge gleaned from country-bred friends and our school botany lessons. It was also an adventure because it always held uncertainty, an exciting adventure because our route through the meadows and lanes surrounding our Leicestershire village must be followed with the greatest stealth, and the hazardous crossing of the railway lines as a short cut was undertaken as a terrifying risk not merely of life and limb, but of parental discovery.

Owing to Nature's frugality in edible fungus, miles of careful search were essential to obtain a reasonable quantity of the breakfast delicacy. Our young, keen eyes would scan a great sweep of dew-wet grass for a glint of white, and having found one we hurried towards it with an uprush of pleasurable anticipation.

The thick, pithy stalk was cut with care, for careless pulling would have brought away the mycelium, the tangled, white thread-like growth below the soil surface, and so destroyed future progeny. The exquisitely delicate deep pink gills radiating from the stalk were examined lest a voracious slug should lurk between them, and then we laid our acquisition on the linen lining our baskets.

The dream we cherished year after year was to find a mushroom ring: to see a circle of deep green turf dotted closely with matt white domes, and to be able to stand within it and fill our baskets to the brim.

This dream was eventually realised, and on this particular day we had risen earlier than ever, tramped along the Lutterworth main road, our wellington boots clumping eerily in the stillness that precedes the dawn, turned into a branching lane and sat astride a field gate waiting for daybreak.

Half an hour later we found the ring. It was about six feet in diameter, the edging band of dark green grass a foot wide and clustered spasmodically with the thrusting heads of button mushrooms and the flat umbrellas of the more mature. We were almost speechless with delight, and danced madly in and out of the circle in a travesty of the dance of fairies to which country folk at one time attributed the growth of a ring.

We filled our baskets to overflowing, leaving the smallest buttons to grow to size, ready for our next visit. It was then, and only then, that Maggie suddenly pointed above our heads and in what can only be described as tones of anguish cried, "*Oh, look! It's an ash!*"

Disappointment bitter as gall swept away the joy and left us dredged, disenchanted and miserable. We could not summon the courage to throw away the innocent-looking contents of our baskets, however violently we felt their perfidy, but made our way sadly homewards.

As we went we waxed sarcastic about the silliness and ignorance of village people who would never eat mushrooms gathered from beneath an ash tree, and scoffed at our own knowledge of poisoning suffered by acquaintances who had ignored this rule.

But the sad truth was that our defiance was vanquished by parental command, and the harvest of the fairy ring deposited on the garden compost heap.

With the passing of time and the resilience of youth, however, we recaptured the thrill of finding the ring and overlooked the sequel. The mounting years can never obscure the magical joy of gathering country mushrooms so far removed from their present-day cultivated cousins in the greengrocer's window.

GEE TENNENT

Michaelmas Daisies

Michaelmas Daisies colour my eye
clustered in colonies, heads in the sky,
wistfully nodding frail petals they dream
of far summer days, warm sunshine with green.
They dance a sad ballet, bow to the breeze,
confined to their blossoming destinies.

Michaelmas Daisies deep rooted in place,
lost in the garden, the last in the race,
destined to temper a cold autumn grey
when gardens surrender in wild disarray;
destined to sacrifice purple with blue
and colour the eyes of the garden anew.

Michaelmas Daisies dance out your lament;
dance for the sweet summer fragrance now spent;
dance ever closer the prelude to doom,
live for the moment, your time follows soon.
Dance in the swirl of a cold winter gale
clinging together so ragged and pale.

SALTER FOX

Do You Remember 1926?

It was more than sixty years ago, but the memories are so fresh in my mind it seems but yesterday — that traumatic event of 1926, the Coal Strike. Dad was a collier, a *daytler*, a man who cleared the muck away from the pit bottom after a fall. That coal strike was a tragedy to our Mam, and many more colliers' wives and families.

Most of the men liked a pint of beer, a pipe of baccy and a bet on the horses, but after the wives had been given their allotted amount of money each week to pay the rent and buy food, there had been little enough left to save for a rainy day. Consequently debts were run up at the little corner shops, with desperate promises made to pay as soon as the strike was ended.

But the strike went on and on for weeks and months.

It was a blessing when the Soup Kitchens were organised. These were usually located in some pub back-yard, the landlord's wife being called upon to help in the preparation of the broth. Bones and scraps were given by the local butchers, vegetables by farmers and allotment holders. A queue would form long before the thick broth was ready, the savoury smell tickling our nostrils as we waited impatiently. Loaves would be cut into thick wedges and handed out along with the jugs and basins of broth. And so little bellies would be filled for another day.

Mam, as did all the colliers' wives, used to bake her own bread. But when the strike came the stocks of coal quickly ran out, and she could not keep a big enough fire going to heat the oven in the black iron fire-grate. So she would knead her bread dough, place it in tins, put a piece of paper on top with our name and address printed on and we kids would take it along to the bakery, where it would be baked for a few pence. Then, a couple of hours later we would have to pick up the cooled tins, hoping the bit of paper was still on top.

"I can't keep going on like this," Mam said. "I can't afford to keep paying the baker." It was a miracle that she could afford to buy flour at all. No wonder Mam looked worried all that summer; no surprise that she was bad tempered.

"You'll have to go coal picking same as t'other kids," she told us. "I've got to have a fire." So off my brother and I went next morning, with the old wooden, canvas-bottomed baby push-chair, a couple of sacks, various small garden tools, some bread and jam and a bottle of water.

After several miles of trudging about, searching, we found a likely spot, at last, where a pit had once stood many years before. We worked away like beavers, scratching, digging, sorting, and after four hours or more had a sack and a half full of a black substance which looked as if it might burn. "Bats", the colliery people called it.

It was while we were resting and eating our "snap" that we saw the apples lying on the ground in a garden close by. "Bet they're juicy," I said to my brother. "Let's get some," was the response. It was the first time I'd ever been scrumping, but it was to be the last.

With our second sack filled to the top with apples, and with one clutched in our fists, we munched our way along to the main road. But we were suddenly accosted by the garden owner. "'Ere, let me look in them sacks," and he dragged one off the push-chair and tipped it up right there outside the church gates! It was the one with the apples in and they were rolling all over the pavement and into the road.

Country Blood

I am of the countryside
Carved out of the oaktree bark
And I am of the wild free wind
That bears the soaring lark.
Part of the upturned earth am I,
One with the cornfield sea,
And I exist in the quiet green hill
And it exists in me.

Here all the dainty weeds are mine
That blow along the way,
And all the little rustling things
Whose hearts beat for a day.
My peace is where the velvet dew
Sleeps under hanging mists;
Where the cavernous forest deeps and dims
My secret soul exists.

J. STURGESS

"What's yer names then, and where does the pair on yer live?" he wanted to know. Then he let us go and we were trembling, and our knees knocking, all the way home.

Another humiliating experience I remember about 1926 was having to go to the "pop shop" (the pawnbrokers). Lots of people we knew had for years resorted to this method of obtaining a bit of quick, ready cash. But not us. Although Mam and Dad were living on the borderline of poverty, having four young mouths to feed, they also had their pride. "What we haven't got we'll do without," Mam used to say.

But things grew worse during those endless weeks. The scraps of food which found their way onto our pantry shelves were eaten the same day, carefully shared out. Men hung about street corners, disconsolate. Their wives gossiped, arms akimbo, sullen, fed up to the teeth, wondering where the next meal was coming from. Then one day Mam had a bundle wrapped up.

"Take this to Starrs," she told us. "Go round the back. Ask him how much he can let you have on it. And be sure to bring the ticket back with you."

Starrs had three big brass balls hanging over the side door . . . the dreaded "pop shop". So, with flushed face and downcast eyes, I departed with the bundle. The man in the musty-smelling back premises looked at me over the top of his glasses. "Mm — not seen you 'ere before," and he took the bundle behind a screen. "I can let yer' ma have ten bob on it," he said as he handed me a ticket and the money.

Mam tut-tutted when she saw the money, but at least we'd be able to eat for the rest of the week. I never did know what had been in that parcel, but Dad did not wear his Sunday suit for a long, long time after that.

Of course it wasn't all gloom and tragedy during those lean months. There was the lighter side; the street football matches, and the miners' cricket teams who played anywhere where there was enough space, and the bathers who crowded the canals. And of course we had Dad at home, to play with us, to go on long walks, to listen to us. But he grew gaunt and sad as the weeks went by.

And then it was all over, sanity restored. There was the familiar ring of hobnailed boots on the pavements; the lists on the slates at the corner shop were gradually erased and Mam started to laugh and sing once more. But over the years it was instilled into me to always save a bit for a rainy day, because, as Mam would say, "You never know."

ELSIE GADSBY

Washday in the 1920s

Sometimes when I switch on my automatic washer, I think of the washdays of my childhood in the 1920s. I see long lines of white-starched clothes, bright gingham dresses and baby clothes flapping in the breeze on lines stretched between the apple trees and rows of towels, tea-towels and other small articles lying on the green grass to bleach in the summer sunshine.

Much preparatory work had been done before this stage in the washday programme was reached. There was no mains water conveniently on tap; the rain water collected from the roof of our farmhouse into tall barrels standing on a high stillage had to be transferred to the lower barrel. This was often a Saturday afternoon task for my father or one of the hired men, as it needed someone tall and strong to bucket the water from one to the other.

On Mondays, winter and summer, at 7.30am a very large jovial woman arrived on her bicycle from a village four miles away. Her first task was to fill the washing boiler and get the fire going. In about half an hour, and for several hours to follow, steam billowed from the washhouse as boilerfuls of clothes were bubbled clean.

The washing programme was long and arduous. Once the water was hot enough, it was ladled from the boiler to a dolly-tub with a one-handled tin or enamel container known as a "lading can". This almost obsolete article was rather like a large cup holding roughly two quarts.

After soap powder had been added the clothes were "possed" with a "posser" (or "posher") — a wooden

shaft to which a wooden disc was attached, an up and down movement being used; or they were agitated with a "dolly", a wooden shaft with projecting arms or legs.

Following this strenuous work the dirty parts were scrubbed with a soft-bristled laundry brush, or rubbed up and down a rubbing board. This consisted of a strip of galvanised corrugated tin attached to a wooden frame. Another possing or dollying in a fresh tub of water and the whites were ready for the boiler, after they had been wrung through the heavy wringer. Whilst the water was heating up, the next lot was tackled using some of the water that had been the second water for the whites.

If there were babies in the house, their clothes were carefully washed separately in fresh water. When I was eight years old I had three smaller sisters, and this meant piles of washing of white cotton dresses trimmed with lace or needlework, cotton underskirts, and print and gingham dresses for me.

When the white clothes had boiled clean they were lifted with a wooden shaft about a yard long into a bucket and dropped into a dolly-tub of clean cold water, agitated or possed, wrung out into a second rinsing water, and lastly into a "blue" water. I used to love trailing my hands through this water and pretending it was the sea.

After all the white clothes came the light-coloured things — my dresses, Mother's aprons, cushion covers and the like, followed by the darker coloureds such as Father's cotton jackets, known locally in those days as "slops". They were usually navy blue or speckled grey, occasionally khaki. Lastly came the stockings, cashmere or cotton socks, Father's thick hand-knitted stockings he wore for work on the farm, his best cashmere socks and mother's light woollen or lisle stockings.

When all the washing was finished any hot water left had to be used, for there was no wasting of this precious commodity in those days. All the milking stools were scrubbed as were shovel and broom handles, the wash-house table and floor were swilled and scrubbed and the flagstones outside the wash-house.

On hot summer days sometimes the starched things dried too much and had to be dampened by sprinkling with water before being folded prior to ironing. This folding was quite a business as such things as towels, flannelette sheets, and tea-towels were not ironed but put through the wringer which made quite a good job of them if two people worked together. The rollers of the old-fashioned wringer were very heavy and if the articles were guided through carefully and slowly they rarely had a crease in them.

Tablecloths, expecially if allowed to dry too much or if they were dried in a wind, often went "out of square" and stayed that way on account of being stiff with starch. When this happened two people holding them by opposite corners had to pull them back into shape. Once the clothes had been folded or rolled up they were ready for ironing, provided they hadn't been allowed to dry out too much. Winter was the worst time as nothing seemed to dry outside. There were no man-made, quick-dry garments then; everything had to be draped over a wooden clothes horse (or "maiden") or on the rack which hung near the kitchen ceiling and could be lowered on a pulley and was a feature of most houses. We, as children, used to hate coming home from school to damp, steamy rooms on wet winter days.

The ironing itself was not just a matter of switching on an electric iron. I remember flat irons which were heated by standing them up in front of the fire and used until they cooled down, when they were reheated. Most people had two or three irons so that there was no waiting. A good flat iron had a smooth shiny bottom, and some housewives used to rub the hot iron with a piece of beeswax wrapped in a cloth to give extra slippiness to the surface. Sometimes flat irons were spoiled by someone carelessly putting them onto the actual fire and allowing the iron to become red hot; this ruined the iron forever and a metal shoe had to be bought to put the iron into once it was heated.

Later on charcoal irons became the thing to have. Heavy and cumbersome after the easily-manipulated flat iron, they nevertheless had the advantage of retaining their heat for much longer. Charcoal was placed in a kind of long-handled wire basket and placed in the fire to become red hot. These glowing pieces were emptied into the iron which was then filled up with more charcoal. The iron was then taken out to a draughty corner such as the end of the house (ours used to stand on a post turned with the opening to the wind) for about ten minutes until all the charcoal was at white heat. It used to be quite exciting to see the sparks flying from it when the charcoal first became ignited, but it was no use bringing the iron back until it was filled with a white-hot glow.

The "box iron" also had its day. Metal heaters were put into the fire until they were red hot and then put into the iron through a little door at the back. They were noisy in use as the heater tended to move about inside the iron, and it also meant having a big fire all the time to keep up a supply of heaters.

The clothes needed a lot of heat to get them up to perfection and most housewives prided themselves on their ironing. All tapes were opened out, lace edgings properly ironed out, pillowcases without a crease — the smell of warm, starched garments was sweet on the air.

Incredibly, that woman who had ridden in on her bicycle at 7.30am was often still hard at work ironing and singing when I went to bed at night. What she would have given for one of our automatics today!

HAZEL COTTAM

Country Fashion

In days gone by,
Once women wed,
They wore a cover
On the head,
In certain places,
To this day,
This ancient custom
Still holds sway.
And widows donned a cap of white,
Not black, to mark their sorry plight.
Great Grandmama was never seen
Without one, goffered, starched and clean,
And in a heavy oaken chest,
She kept her veil and wedding dress,
Her shift and stockings laid beside,
To be her shroud, the day she died.
Grandma had one hat, of straw,
(She kept it in a pillow-case)
Highdays and holidays she wore
It decked with ribbons, flowers and lace.
Each Spring she'd furbish it anew,
With peacock feathers, change the trim,
Then with writing ink of blue,
She'd brighten up the faded brim.

DOROTHY MARY WADE

Going Shopping

OPEN

As a small boy it used to be one of my greatest pleasures to go shopping with my mother on a Saturday morning. Around about ten o'clock, I used to be put into my best suit (a sailor suit of which I was extremely proud), then off we would set for the shops, which were about a mile away.

The first visit was always to the Penny Bazaar to enable me to spend my weekly pocket money — one whole penny! This was always a most serious business; much could be bought for a penny in those days. Then we would go to "Burge-the-Fishmonger".

Although I did not care for all the fish staring at me with their glassy eyes from the midst of their nests of melting ice, there were lots of other interesting things to see — scarlet lobsters, and fierce-looking crabs. Sometimes there was even a bowl of eels, all tangled up, and looking as though they might slither onto the floor at any moment.

Next came "Hall's-the-Grocers". This was a great favourite of mine. I can still remember the wonderful smell of cheese, bacon, and the sawdust on the floors, with sometimes, over-ruling the lot, the glorious aroma of roasting coffee.

Buying cheese here was a great ceremony. Mr. Hall himself would serve us personally. Producing an instrument consisting of a shiny tube with a wooden handle, he would plunge the tube into a cheese selected by Mother, then withdraw it, bringing with it a thin cylinder of

cheese, which a movement of the handle would extrude from the end of the cylinder like tooth-paste.

Mother would then break off a piece and taste it, and of course I would do the same. On a good day we might sample as many as five or six different cheeses like this.

There was also a lady who, when asked, would with the aid of a pair of funny-looking wooden bats, dig out a lump from a huge block of butter and after slapping it and smacking it, tossing it in the air and catching it again, within minutes would produce a neat square of butter, which when placed on the shiny brass scales was always exactly the weight asked for, and which never had to have bits added to or taken away from it. I always hoped one day to see her drop it on the floor, but she never did.

In this shop there was a system of wires, each one starting several feet above each of the various counters, and all leading up to a small glass-sided office, high above the floor at one end of the shop. Here sat a huge fat lady, for all the world like a great fat spider in the middle of her web, and at first I used to shudder, and think that she sat there waiting to grab anyone who became entangled in her wires.

When we had paid for our purchases the bill and the money were placed in a little jar-like container, which was then fixed to the underside of one of the little trollies, which were suspended from these wires. Mr. Hall then pulled a handle of the contraption, which catapulted the trolley up to Mrs. Spider, as I thought of her. A moment or two later, the trolley would run back to us along the wire and Mr. Hall would open the container and give us our change.

One great day, when I had grown out of my fear of Mrs. Spider and things were quiet in the shop, I was lifted up onto the counter, and allowed to pull the handle, but alas I was not strong enough to catapult the trolley all the way back to the office, hard though I tried.

Next we often visited one or other of the various milliners' shops, but these did not interest me much. However, there was always the chance of meeting more of my mother's friends in these, one or two of whom were particular favourites of mine, as they always seemed to be able to find a sweet or chocolate in the depths of their handbags!

If I had been good, our final visit was always to "Harry-n-Woods". This was a small tea-shop run by two old ladies of those names. Here mother would have a cup of coffee with cream in it, and a cake or two, and I would have a tall glass of fizzy lemonade and a lemon bun, the top of the latter all prickly with sugar. Occasionally I would have a Chelsea bun, when the great game would be to see how much of it I could unwind without it breaking.

It would now be time to go home. Usually we walked,

but occasionally if we had a lot of parcels to carry we would take a Hansom Cab. This was always a great thrill. I would clamber up the high steps into the cab, aided by a push behind from mother, then when she had also got in the driver would close the heavy, curved

wooden doors over our knees, climb up to his perch high above the back of the cab, and with a shake of the reins and a crack of the whip, off we would rattle.

In these strange vehicles, the only means of communication between the driver and his fares was through the small glass trap door, and when under way the noise from the horse's hooves, and that of the steel-tyred wheels on the stone setts, with which the town roads were surfaced in those days, was such that conversation was almost impossible.

The passengers could see out of the glass windows in the sides of the cab, and they had a magnificent view out of the front of the cab, a view however which was mostly filled by the horse's hindquarters, at any rate as far as a small boy was concerned.

Almost invariably before we reached home the horse would lift its tail, always well docked so as not to swish the passengers in the face, and mother would suddenly say: "Frank, hold your breath!" This I would do at once, holding my breath until I was red in the face, and almost bursting, but I never succeeded in doing so long enough!

But it was all part of the fun of going shopping. FRANK RAILTON

THE OLD APPLE ROOM

Whenever I smell the sweet, indescribable scent of ripe apples I am transported back to my grandfather's farm. Once again I am in the airy room of the Essex farmhouse where the apples were stored. Hand-picked, only the perfect specimens individually wrapped in old newspaper were taken to the apple room in October to be used throughout the winter. Even in the spring, when every single one of the crisp delicious fruit had been eaten and the room lay empty, a faint reminder of apples lingered in the air.

Grandfather was, as my aunt who kept house for him never failed to remark, a "gentleman farmer". The distinction merely meant that he was fortunate enough to be the owner of five farms, working one and renting out the rest to tenants.

By the time I knew him, Grandfather's sight was deteriorating and he was too old to lead a very active life. Nevertheless, although he had four strapping adult sons, he still held the reins. Each morning the farm hands gathered in the yard close to the house. At 6.30 an upstairs window jerked open with a bang, and grandfather appeared in his nightshirt. His hands were always raised above his head to hold the window frame in case the sash-cord broke. He looked out, but he could not always discern whether all his men were outside, or not. The routine never varied; one by one they addressed him: "G'morning, Mr. Musselwhite," and with each one — Tom, Will, Ned — he exchanged a greeting. Then he gave them their orders for the day, let down the window, and retired.

Later in the morning he would come downstairs and if it was dry would sit out of doors on an upright chair. Sometimes he sat in the hedged garden under the monkey-puzzle tree. But best of all he liked to be settled by the back door, listening to and watching the white hens as they kept up their companionable clucking around the yard. If anyone asked him why he had no Rhode Island Reds or Buff Orpingtons on the farm, pride prompted him to say White Leghorns were the better layers, though the truth was that white birds were now the only ones he could distinguish.

To me, collecting the eggs was the greatest fun. In those days, when batteries were unheard of, the hens roamed freely all over the place. The egg-laying habits of Grandfather's White Leghorns were decidedly untidy and the daily gathering of the eggs was the nearest thing to a game of hide and seek. Having first emptied the hen houses my sister and I never knew where else we might come across an egg or two, hidden in the hedgerow, in the barns, or discreetly bedded in the long grass of the orchard.

On warm afternoons we were allowed to take a picnic to the orchard. Hedges were at that time an integral part of the East Anglian landscape, and the thick thorn hedge enclosing the orchard, leaving only a gap for the white wicket gate, turned into a secretive, sheltered retreat. Often we played there till the cowman, Ned, called to us from the lane as he drove the cows homes to be milked.

"Our milk," Grandfather told us more than once,

"goes to Southend." The heavy pails of creamy milk in the cowsheds were later transferred into the tall, shiny milk churns inscribed EDWARD MUSSELWHITE and delivered to Shenfield station to be sent by the milk train all the way to the coast. Not actually very far, but Southend was beside the sea; to a child in that flat Essex countryside, the sea seemed a long way off.

Grandfather was a strict Protestant, a God-fearing man. While staying with him we were not allowed to play games on Sundays, not even such harmless pastimes as Solitaire, or Snakes and Ladders. So whenever possible we were taken for an afternoon walk. My aunt had a countrywoman's knowledge of the wild life of field and hedgerow, and from her we learnt the names of all the wild flowers growing within miles of the farm. The golden coltsfoot, first herald of the spring, dog's-mercury and cuckoo-pint, green and inconspicuous, glossy-leaved celandine, vetch, trefoil, St. John's wort, with all these and dozens more we became familiar. We searched along the field edges for the tiny scarlet pimpernel "the poor man's weather-clock", opening and closing its vivid petals in obedience to the sun. And in a world as yet unaware of the need for conservation, we carried back bunches of violets, primroses, wood anemones and cowslips, which, I sadly recall, frequently drooped in our hands before we reached home.

If wet, there was no alternative but to sit, dressed in our "Sunday best", in the drawing room where a portrait of Great Grandmamma, magnificently framed if poorly painted, kept a stern eye upon us. There we spent the dullest hours of the week, turning over the pages of an immense scrapbook our father had compiled as a boy. I have it still; a handsome volume, bound in green leather. Today, it being a tangible remembrance of things past, I find the elaborate scraps absorbing. As a child I fidgeted over them, longing for Hannah to come and light the oil lamps and tell us tea was ready.

Leading out of the kitchen was the scullery, where the pump was housed. It drew water from a well which "had never been known to run dry". A supply was drawn up, as far as I remember, twice a day by Hannah, the maid. Poor Hannah, it must have been a thankless task on a bitter January morning, for even by midday the warmth of the kitchen rarely managed to penetrate the chilly scullery, with its brick floor and door opening directly on to the yard. But Hannah was a cheerful soul, she did not complain. On our visits she carried a heavy jug of hot water upstairs to our bedroom each morning, so that we might wash from the bowl on the marble washstand.

Though a sizeable farmhouse, it had no such luxury as a bathroom, but there was an indoor loo. To reach it entailed a walk down a long passage lined with books. Once through the door at the far end, one was confronted not only by the objective of the journey, but also by pile upon pile of old magazines stacked in neat array around the floor. The delight of it was that they were mostly old copies of *Punch*, which turned it into a highly entertaining expedition!

Memory is selective; much else has faded into oblivion. Before my ninth birthday, we moved north to a large industrial town. Our visits to the farm ceased. But each Christmas a wooden barrel arrived from Essex. When it was opened I put my hand inside, knowing that after a brief exploration of its bran-filled interior I would discover an apple, first one, then another, and another. Though far from Grandfather's farm, our home, too, temporarily harboured the delicate fragrance of "apples wond'rous ripe".

ELIZABETH ROYSTON

Cycling to court

In 1906, when I was 14 years old, I had been at work full time for two years. In this time I had, by diligence and hard work, caused my wage to be raised from five to six shillings per week, and also realised my great ambition — to own a bicycle. I had saved 19 shillings and needed only one more to achieve the price at which it had been offered, but I could wait no longer. I went to the owner and said that I had 19 shillings and that, if I could have the machine, I would bring him the balance on my next pay day.

I well remember his comment "You don't want to buy a bike, my boy, you want to beg one!" My face must have betrayed my feelings because he added: "Go on! Take it away. Forget the shilling and take it easy now. No record breaking."

I loved that machine. I cleaned and oiled it almost daily. I stood and admired it for minutes together. I saved up and bought a speedometer which worked from the front wheel. It was bolted onto a fork and engaged with a small pawl on a spoke, making a pleasant click with each revolution. This enabled me to watch the little counter registering the mileage as I rode. I saved again and bought, for 5s 9d, a Lucas Acetylene lamp. It was of highly-polished electroplate and threw a powerful beam when a chamber filled with crystals became damp, as water dripped on them from another chamber.

I rode it through all the horse traffic in the centre of Birmingham to places like Warwick and Leamington, and for tours of the delightful "leafy lanes". It was all

mine! Bought and paid for by the sweat of the brow. Then, abruptly, it all ended.

I was riding down a hill near the centre of the city, following a horse-drawn van which rather quickly pulled to a stop. I went round the van to avoid hitting it and I am not sure what happened next. I seemed to float on air with the buildings sinking down, and I found myself sitting, dazed, in the mud by my bicycle.

A short distance away a massive policeman, easily the largest I had ever seen, was rising to a standing position. He then walked about two yards and picked up his spinning helmet. He was covered with mud, except for his

bright red hair. He next approached me and gave me a long and detailed account of how he felt about me. I remember something about not being safe on anything but my mother's clothes-horse and, even then, not outside the kitchen. As I say, it was a long speech, in an accent which I have since recognised as Irish. It drew a vast audience as it was the time when the workers in the jewellery district of Birmingham walked home in droves to the midday meal.

When he had calmed down he asked me if I was hurt. I said "No, Sir." Next I looked at my machine to see if that was hurt, whilst the policeman waited. As I looked a plan formed. If only I could get a leg over the saddle and away, neither he nor anyone in the crowd could catch me. It did not occur to me that I would have to force a path through the crowd; also that I would have to come the same way home every day and would soon be recognised. However, this did not matter because just as I was pretending to be testing the pedals to see that the drive wheel was not damaged, a massive hand came down on the handlebars and the policeman started another speech. "Don't be in any hurry!" he said. "We've got a way of teaching people like you how to ride."

My name and address were taken down, the book and pencil were returned to pocket, the crowds began to fade as quickly as it had formed. I was told to go, and I went. In a week I had forgotten the matter and so, I assumed, had the law.

I was wrong. About two weeks after my encounter with the policeman I received a summons to appear at the court in the centre of Birmingham. I knew then that he had not forgiven me. I got plenty of advice as to what was likely to happen to me. It boiled down to an understanding that I would have to pay a large fine or go to prison.

I soon got over the shock of knowing that I was now outside the law. I planned a firm course of action. First I sold my cycle to have money to pay my fine. I decided to conduct my own defence and wrote out a speech which I felt would reduce the judge and jury almost to tears. I memorised this speech until I was word-perfect.

I brushed my Sunday suit and boots, which were also my working suit and boots, my face and hands shone and I arrived at court well before the stated time. It happened to be Monday. Proceedings started with a procession of weekend drunks. They all knew the drill and were in and out of the dock with the speed and precision of a well-oiled machine.

Now it was my turn. My last-minute silent run over my speech was cut short by the judge, whom I now know to have been a magistrate. He seemed to have some difficulty in finding me and asked, in a kindly voice, if I had a mother or someone else with me. I stood on tiptoe and replied "No, Sir." My crime was read out, my

TEAM WORK

It's quite all right —
this flower is yours
as much as mine.
So carry on
your buzzing song.
Don't mind my fingers
tugging weeds
or sowing seeds —
we know we both
have jobs
that must be done.

No need for me to worry
you might sting.
No need for you to fear
that I'd do anything
to hurt you.
So moving, touching,
in our mutual love
for flowers,
we'll work together,
sing together,
through these precious
sunny hours.

CYNTHIA HAFELI-WELLS

policeman gave his case, and I was asked if I had anything to say.

My confidence returned and I soon warmed up. I explained that I had sold my cycle so that I would never again hit a policeman. I had gone round the van, which had stopped too quickly, to save hitting the back of it. I was just coming to the meat of my defence and had got as far as "the fact that neither the policeman, myself, nor my machine had been injured suggested that I was not riding too fast," when a gentleman sitting below the judge broke in with "fiddlesticks".

The judge spoke; "Five shillings seven days next," a kindly policeman said, "This way, Sonny," five shillings changed hands, and I left the court a free citizen. But the red-haired constable have been right — the fine certainly taught me how to ride a bicycle in the future.

T.J. ASPLEY

A TREASURY

These are the things that make me dream
Of England on a summer's day —
The meadows soft beneath the sun,
A village green where children play,
The shadow'd lawns in morning light,
A heavy dew upon the grass,
A blackbird singing in the dawn,
The sudden whirr of wings that pass;
Then hammock chairs upon the lawn,
And strawberries and cream for tea,
The distant sound of mowing grass,
The nearer hum of passing bee.
And in the mind so richly stored
Are scents that breathe a summer's day —
The smell of earth soon after rain,
The strange, sweet tang of new-mown hay,
And honeysuckle, mint and sage
Seem part of our long heritage;
And when the twilight lingers still,
And day draws softly to a close,
All loveliness seems gathered deep
Within a perfect English rose.

MURIEL HILTON

A Village Christmas

Preparing for Christmas when I was a young schoolgirl in an Oxfordshire village was a very exciting time. For weeks beforehand our mothers and grandmothers would start collecting together the various ingredients for the good things we would have to eat during the festive season. Mincemeat had to be made, also the Christmas cake, and puddings had to be mixed and steamed for hours.

As children we loved to be around in the kitchen at this time because a taste of the raisins (which we helped to stone) and other dried fruits was too good a chance to miss, and it was customary to have a "lucky stir" and toss in the small silver threepenny pieces, one of which we hoped would be in our slice of pudding on Christmas Day. When the cake was ready to be iced and decorated we were allowed to watch, and loved to see the tiny figures of either Father Christmas or traditional Snowman being placed on the top, while our Mother piped the words "Merry Christmas" in coloured icing.

The chicken or turkey had to be ordered from the butcher well in advance, also bacon for boiling or pork for roasting, according to what our families could afford, but of course living in the country in those days, many families kept their own chickens.

We actually made most of our presents for members of the family. These were usually items such as calendars, ironholders, coal gloves, needle-cases, bookmarks, or

coloured woollen balls if there was a new baby in the house. Christmas cards would also be made and packed up with the presents, and these would be carefully hidden away until nearer the holiday time. Packets of multi-coloured gummed paper strips were purchased and these we made into paper chains, together with lanterns made from gummed paper squares. One or two special decorations were purchased and kept from year to year, usually red or green paper bells or large coloured balls. Decorations were also made for the Christmas tree — little crêpe paper bags which we stitched together to be filled with nuts and sweets; paper flowers; and the star for the top of the tree was made by cutting out the shape in cardboard then covering it with silver paper. Some children preferred to have a fairy at the top of their tree and one of these could be bought quite cheaply at Woolworth's or at the Autumn Fair.

The school term usually ended a few days before Christmas Eve, and this time would be busily spent looking for holly, ivy and other greenery with which to decorate our houses, and lastly the tree would be planted in a tub or bucket to be brought indoors on the morning of Christmas Eve. We would cover the bucket with crêpe paper, then trim the tree with all the things we had made. This was one of our happiest occupations. Carefully we would tie on the coloured glass balls, add the sparkling silver tinsel, fix on the metal clip candle-holders with their tiny twisted green, red and white candles, and last of all one of us would climb on a chair to fix the star to the top of the tree. A few small presents would be tied on the tree for us to give to friends, such as pink and white sugar mice, chocolate figures of Father Christmas and chocolate bells and balls.

Carol singers would often call at our house during the week before Christmas, and as they were always known to us we would ask them to come indoors for a warm drink and a mince-pie, ending the evening by all singing together "We wish you a Merry Christmas and a Happy New Year." The Christmas service at our chapel was always a happy one, as the young children acted the story of the Nativity and everyone joined in singing the well-loved carols.

Before going to bed on Christmas Eve we would tell each other stories, or perhaps a favourite one would be read to us whilst sitting in the firelight watching the "soot fairies" dancing their way up the chimney. We would then run eagerly upstairs, get undressed, hang our stockings on the end of the bed and snuggle between the sheets, each determined to stay awake and see Father Christmas creep in — but somehow he always managed to come when our eyes were tightly closed!

In the early hours of Christmas morning lights would be switched on and stockings eagerly taken down and emptied of their contents. Of course we would have some parcels which would not fit into the stockings, but these would be opened later around the tree. One of the favourite gifts at this time was a Sweet Shop made of cardboard, with a tiny stand-up counter on which we placed miniature bottles of sweets for sale, together with a tiny pair of scales, and we would spend many happy hours "buying and selling" (and tasting too, of course!) Another gift might be a Christmas stocking made out of net, which contained many small items such as a toy trumpet or whistle, packet of Dolly Mixtures, a comb, coloured pencils, and a small metal frog which could be clicked between the fingers.

If you were very lucky there would be one special present, and the one I remember receiving was a huge cracker in a long cardboard box. The cracker was beautifully made of pale blue crêpe paper with silver trimmings, and had a spray of darker blue velvet flowers in the centre tied with ribbon. It was a long time before the cracker was carefully opened and its contents removed with exclamations of pleasure and surprise, and later it was sealed up again and replaced in its box, to be brought out again the following year and used as part of the decorations.

It was customary to spend Christmas Day and Boxing Day with our family, but afterwards we would have a party for friends of our own age, and after a scrumptious tea of trifle, jellies, sandwiches, cakes and mince-pies, we would each be given a cracker. These would be quickly pulled amidst much laughter, the mottoes read and paper hats put on, and after the tea-things had been cleared away we would spend an hour or so playing games — Musical Chairs, Postman's Knock, Hunt the Thimble,

Blindman's Buff, Pass the Parcel, Twist the Trouncer (usually Mother's bread board), and of course our very favourite game Charades. All too soon it was time for our friends to go, and as they did so each one would be given either a small parcel, or some fruit, nuts and sweets to take home.

The Christmas celebrations were now over, and on Twelfth Night we carefully took down the decorations from our rooms and tree. These would be packed away in a box ready for use the following year. We took the tree out in the garden and planted it, hoping it would grow, and for weeks afterwards would see tiny tinsel strands shining on its branches — a happy reminder of the Christmas festivities we shared with our family and friends.

To the children of today possibly the simple pleasures of our youth seem trivial, but we were very happy and I think in making our own presents and decorations for Christmas we gained much more satisfaction than if we had had the money to purchase everything from the shops.

PAULINE GRAIN

Song of the Donkey

Why should it happen to me
To be there when He was born;
To see what kings were keen to see
And prophets to forewarn?

Why should it happen to me
To greet Him with my brays,
When others might more tunefully
Have greeted Him with praise?

Why should it happen to me
To bend low over His bed,
And with my rough breathing, warmly
Halo the Infant's head?

Why should it happen to me
To bear on my back His weight,
And share with the Refugee
His cruel winter's flight?

Why should it happen to me
To walk the triumphal way,
That He should say "I have need of thee,
My friend of yesterday"?

And how can we humans, Lord,
Share your Nativity,
Except in obedience to your word
And a donkey's humility?

HARRY BROUGHTON

Easter Memories

Although I have lived overseas for almost thirty years, when I think of Easter it is still the spring flowers of the English countryside that come first to my mind. I can still picture the little grey stone Cornish church where we used to worship. Set below wooded hills, beside banks of pale wild daffodils, Lent-lilies we called them, this church must have seen so many Easter Sundays, so many generations come to give thanks for Easter's good tidings.

On Easter morning the bell-ringers, rosy-faced from exertion, sleeves rolled up, rang an extra joyful peal from the square belfry tower. The bells rang out over the hamlets and scattered farms, calling the people to come together at this glad time. It is as such a joyous day that I remember those Easters, long past, when we gambolled along the country lanes, like the new lambs on the moorland pastures. Early bluebells speared up between the fronds of fresh green bracken beside the paths, chaffinches called as they flew up the lanes before us, while admonishments followed us, urging us to keep our socks clean and our new straw hats in position.

As we neared the church we walked along a woodland ride, where the translucent green of young beech leaves met overhead, while beside the track tiny veined bells of wood-sorrel grew below the great rhododendron bushes, whose fat buds gave promise of the lovely white, rose or lilac flowers to come. The ancient Celtic cross in the churchyard stood with its weathered granite foot in a bed of primroses, and a little bush of sweet-smelling daphne grew beside the moss-grown coffin-rest. The church was always beautifully decorated with daffodils and palm, as we called the sprays of sallow willow, with their haze of golden pollen. Even the musty scents of ancient woodwork and damp stone, varnish and furniture polish, were held at bay by the perfume of the narcissi round the font.

So it is no wonder to me that the early Christian missionaries to the northern countries took over the pagan festival held at the spring of the year, in honour of the Teutonic dawn goddess *Eostre*, from whose name our word Easter comes. They found that the Resurrection of Christ with its tidings of hope and joy could be understood by those who had celebrated the new birth and upsurge of life as personified by *Eostre*, after the dormancy of the northern winter.

Thinking of Easter flowers, and the flower-decked English countryside, reminds me of the last Easter I spent in England, still so fresh in my memory. It was during the last war, when I spent my leave helping in the YMCA canteen aboard HMS *Heron*, a naval training establishment set in the fields of Somerset. It was a novelty to have one's life regulated by ships' bells, and to go aboard the "liberty boat", the bus which took us to the nearest town. Each evening we had to "darken ship", which meant draw the black-out curtains, and the call "up spirits" went out each noon for the men to collect their rum ration. Here came shipwrecked survivors to await redrafting, Wrens employed folding and packing parachutes, Fleet Air Arm crews and a host of others.

The canteen was always crowded; we were rushed off our feet making sandwiches, serving endless cups of tea,

followed by mountains of dishes to be washed, and the long bar-counter to be polished. In addition I found myself a job just to my liking, which was to keep the tables supplied with flowers, which gave a much-needed touch of home and seemed to be appreciated. This entailed cycling along the Somerset lanes, heavy with the scent of blackthorn blossom, and bringing back baskets of cowslips and lady's-smocks to arrange in little glass fish-paste jars. At Eastertime I persuaded a local farmer to let me raid his garden in a good cause, picking big bunches of white and purple lilac with which to decorate the canteen. Almost my last sight before leaving HMS *Heron* was of Hugh of the Naval Film Unit, going on leave to his home in heavily-blitzed London, taking his young wife two sprays of lily-of-the-valley carefully wrapped in tissue-paper, tucked inside his naval jumper. Easter for me will always mean spring flowers, with their message of joy and hope.

DOREEN BARFIELD

NOWADAYS

In the golden maze of the dear old days,
There was time enough and to spare,
The world was new and love was true,
Men brave and maidens fair.
A rose grown cot was the happy lot
Of the bridegroom and his bride
And a garden gay with a primrose way,
And a moss-garden well beside.

But we're past all that, and five-room flat
Is the home of the modern pair,
No driftwood's light on the hearth at night,
But a gas-stove's glittering glare.
No more he waits at the garden gates,
While she comes through the gloaming pale
She comes with much fuss on a motor 'bus
To list to the old, old tale.

He brings no flowers fresh from fragrant showers,
That he's gathered in the dell,
But flowers coy by a messenger boy
He sends his love to tell.
He proposes by wire in words of fire —
Twelve little words alone;
And she whispers "yes", as you may guess,
Over the telephone!

C. HOLMES

Harvest Holiday

As the waggon swayed and jolted over the wellum I clung to the top for dear life. I must concentrate on nodding and shaking my head in the right places. As old Benin chattered away in his Essex dialect he must never guess that I understood only one word in three.

Nearly 50 years have passed, but that scene from my childhood is still vividly before me: the lean, grizzled old farm-worker, his trouser legs tied round with binder twine; the smell of sweat from the horses; the feeling of mingled triumph and terror as we ducked to avoid the overhanging apple boughs which threatened to sweep us from our lofty perch as we rocked home along the orchard path.

Harvest on my uncle's farm had begun some weeks before. Together we had pushed the ancient Massey-Harris binder out of its shed, brushed off the hens' droppings, checked the canvases and threaded the twine. Thanks to a "lucky shilling" concealed in its works, the faithful old machine kept going pretty well, but occasionally it threw a temperamental fit and left sheaf after sheaf untied — usually the thistly ones.

But before we could use the binder a swath had to be cut round the outside of the field with a scythe, and I had to come behind to tie up the loose corn with straw bands. Laid crops also had to be cut by hand, for the binder could not pick them up, and a storm when the harvest was ripe meant hours of back-breaking work.

My main job was stooking, and I soon learnt that there is an art in it. Each sheaf must be banged down firmly with the knot facing the right way, otherwise the whole erection will collapse before you are out of the field. There should be six or eight sheaves to a stook: to my uncle's annoyance visiting "helpers", given half a chance, would build enormous stooks of ten or twelve sheaves, which took ages to dry out.

While we stooked, the binder worked towards the centre of the field in ever-decreasing rectangles. When it had almost reached the middle, as if by magic, men and boys with lurchers at their heels and sticks in their hands would appear and gather round the patch of corn which was still standing, waiting for the rabbits cowering there to run out. I hated this slaughter, and wished my uncle would forbid it. I would continue resolutely with my stooking, but a sudden shout would make me turn my head and a brown, furry body would streak past, eyes wild, ears laid back, pursued by dogs and men. If I could, I would get in the way of the pursuers, but I could seldom do much good. Someone would return in triumph holding up the limp, warm body by the back legs and then lay it under a sheaf to stiffen.

In time an old Fordson replaced the horses, and when it came to carting my job was to drive the tractor, a task I hated. The "old lady" was very hard to turn and, no matter how much I tried not to crash her gears, she would emit grating groans which made my uncle glare. I had no skill in building a load: my erections would wobble dangerously in spite of all my efforts to lay the sheaves on the cart neatly with the butts out. If I was on the waggon, Uncle usually played safe and came back with half the normal load.

At threshing time there was no room at all for amateur help. The thresher arrived with the contractor's own gang, mostly Irishmen, tanned and quick-tongued, and all day long the stackyard was filled with flying chaff and the whirr and throb of the machine. My task was confined to carrying huge jugs of syrupy tea into the dim, sweet-smelling barn, where relays of men took a few minutes off from the heat and dust of the stack. After three days of incessant activity the threshing was finished. The machine would be taken away, we would drag up the heavy green covers to protect the stacks until the thatcher could come, and all would be quiet again.

This was really the end of summer. Uncle would take the tractor and plough down to Paradise and cut rich brown furrows across the golden stubble. One or two gleaners would ask permission to work over Longstones before he ploughed that up. Already there was a nip in the air, and in the mornings the spiders' webs were silvered with tiny drops. Another week and school would begin again. My harvest holiday was almost over for another year.

BETTY MORRIS

PROGRESS?

Miss Meacham kept the baker's shop
Opposite the green by the village bus stop,
Everyone loved her — what a dear,
A vague sweet memory of yesteryear;
The shop was the target of village boys
As gloriously,
Uproariously
They raced from school midst dust and noise
To the shop which held my childhood joys.

Miss Meacham's shop, they always said,
Would stand there till the village was dead;
No spicy buns ever tasted so sweet,
No shop shelves ever kept so neat;
And stocked with iced-cake, custard tart,
So beautifully,
Dutifully,
In our old village, played her part
This dear soul with the tender heart.

But now I stand and stare at the spot
Where city gents took over the lot;
I've been abroad for seven years,
And see the village through mist of tears:
No shop with smell of fresh-baked bread,
For drastically,
Fantastically,
A supermarket stands instead;
Miss Meacham's shop, they always said,
Would remain until the village was dead.

HILDA GEE

The Sunday Outing

Through London's thick yellow fog, a clanking, rattling Monster could be heard approaching the place where we were standing, outside the Blackwall Tunnel entrance in Poplar by the West India Dock. The tram — a double deck, open top, red-painted, swaying conveyance — screeched to a halt on the slippery rails, its one headlight fighting against the thick pea-souper that was enveloping us.

I climbed aboard and sat on the long seat that ran the length of the tram, taking in the strong smell of disinfectant that met one's nostrils. These trams seemed to be sprinkled regularly with the stuff. I liked to sit immediately behind the driver who, standing outside by his levers, stamped his foot hard on the bell and gleaming in wet oilskins set this wonderful, thrilling, noisy thing in motion.

It was a Sunday afternoon and having been scrubbed with carbolic soap, and dressed in our Sunday Best, despite the weather, my Father was taking my brother (aged two) and myself (aged five) up to Liverpool Street station to see the Locomotive Trains. This was our weekly outing, and a real adventure, to which we eagerly looked forward. I think the fare was about tuppence return, and the *ting* of the conductor's ticket punch was an added tune to our outing.

We lived in my great-grandmother's house in Poplar. It had two floors, a semi-basement, and a lot of people who wanted forty winks on a Sunday afternoon. So here we were clanking our way along the East India Dock Road to Gardener's Corner at Aldgate East. Our driver kept banging his foot on the bell every few minutes as we swayed along the tracks, over the junctions and points, shouting out to people who were walking along the tracks, or to a horse and cart which might be getting in the way.

Although he had a chain across the entrance at his end, he would often let people climb aboard who happened to be on the wrong side of the track, when the tram stopped. It wasn't allowed, of course, but in those days everything seemed to be so much more jolly and people more friendly. At Gardener's Corner we dismounted from the tram in the middle of the road on a small island, and then gingerly crossed the slippery cobblestoned road, passed Aldgate Underground station, and then to Houndsditch, where the wholesale businesses were. We would walk along this road until we came to Bishopsgate, and there was the Railway Station. The entrance doorways were dimly lit with spluttering gas mantles; there always seemed to be hurrying people going backwards and forwards.

We used to like going round to the front entrance and down the long slope, which was used by the taxis, and which gave access to the trains going to Ipswich and King's Lynn, etc, and of course "the Hook of Holland".

There always seemed to be a train standing with Pullman and Buffet cars on the platform, which stretched right back into the dark of the station. This platform gave access to the train without going through a barrier and we used to stand under the bridge which linked platforms, looking at the huge arrival and departure boards displaying faraway places, such as Felixstowe or Lowestoft or Cromer, and wishing for a place on the train. It was wonderful to walk slowly along beside the train, looking at the little red-shaded lamps in the dining cars, and watching the porters struggling with trolley loads of luggage, and passengers carrying travelling rugs hurrying along behind.

Then we would be down at the very end of the platform, standing beside a huge Green Monster with the letters LNER emblazoned on its flanks. This engine would be gleaming with polished pipes and oiled steel parts, the steam coming out at various places, and the whole thing being alive, seemingly full of vitality, pulsating with a steady beat ready to surge forward at the touch of the driver's hand. We could see in the driver's cab, and watch the fireman stoking up, amazed at the tons of coal in the tender that would be shifted by this man to keep the steam pressure up. The driver would be seen with his long oil-can lubricating a hidden connection, and occasionally looking at his huge pocket watch. All railwaymen seemed to carry huge watches on chains — whether the railway provided them or not I never did find out.

Twice I was extremely lucky. An uncle of mine was a fireman, and I was helped into the cab, sat on the driver's perch, shown the driving lever which opened the throttle, and saw where the whistle cord was, felt the heat and vibration, smelled the hot oil and steam, and vowed I would be an engine-driver when I grew up. We would stand and watch the hurrying throng die away, then hear a distant whistle; we could see the guard in the middle of the train waving his green flag, and then another railway official near the engine would raise his hand to the driver and either blow a whistle or yell our "Right Away."

Then it would happen, a shrieking piercing whistle, a noise so loud we would stuff our fingers in our ears, enjoying the thrill of it, then a reverberating *whoosh, shoosh*, roar and shudder, as all-enveloping steam escaped from down round the wheels. And with a huge groan, the giant slowly moved forward, the huge wheels slithering to get a grip on the rails, as the terrific strain was taken up. We would always wave to the driver, who waved back and in my eyes was the hero of the hour. Visitors and passengers would be waving to one another, calling out last-minute farewells. I would stand entranced as each carriage slipped by, going a little faster than the one in front as the train gained momentum, each carriage being counted, and the grand total being shouted over and over again.

We would joyously walk back along the deserted platform to our next excitement, climbing and counting the steps up to the connecting bridge which ran across the rails to the platforms over the other side of the station, where the trains going to Southend and Shenfield started from. We would stand on this bridge waiting for a long express from a distant shore to come in slowly under our feet, and stop to empty its passengers. Little did I dream then that years later I would come in on those expresses, in uniform to a blacked-out station.

We had to inspect all the engines which were standing in the station, and then sadly but happily we would begin the walk to Aldgate for our return tram journey, wondering what adventure we would have next Sunday. Our last thrill for the day was to listen to the barrel-organ being played near the tram stop, giving a penny to the man turning the handle. I can hear the tunes now in memory . . . but it seems many lifetimes ago.

RON COLLIER